A BIGGER PIECE OF BLUE

A Bigger Piece of Blue

STORIES

Dan T. Cox

This is a work of fiction. Names, characters, places, organizations and incidents either are the product of the author's imagination or are used fictionally, and any resemblance to actual persons, living or dead, events, or locales is entirely coincidental.

ISBN: 1548733962
ISBN 13: 9781548733964
Library of Congress Control Number: 2017910853
CreateSpace Independent Publishing Platform
North Charleston, South Carolina

For Mike McClain

CONTENTS

ACKNOWLEDGEMENTS

THE AUTHOR RESPECTFULLY THANKS THOSE who helped to lure these stories out of the woods. Three beta readers did the heavy lifting, scrutinizing the words with intelligent, honest, insightful eyes—Kandee McClain, Kelley Baker, and Mike McClain. Shannon Wilson, Paul Warnock, Marigrace Cohen, Erica Witbeck, Debra Warnock, Matt Cohen, and Cynthia Gladen, PhD., provided additional observations. Hats off to the cover design by Stephanie Murphy. Deep appreciation to noted illustrator Michael Schwab for the original cover art. A second thank-you goes to Kelley Baker for his persistent encouragement over the years to get these stories into print. Special thanks are reserved for Gayle Hannahs, who in addition to lending her literary insights, created a new life with the author that made it possible for him to return to the challenges of rewriting stories until they are good enough to share. Finally, thanks go to the educators who shaped a once-young, aspiring writer—This list includes Mike McClain, who taught the writer to write; Helen Cox, the author's grammar-conscious mom; and Professor William J. Handy, PhD., whose fascination with the likes of Updike, Joyce, Faulkner, Hemingway, Malamud, and Bellow was contagious.

I'm comfortable with dust and practical as gravel.

—Creighton Bliss

A Bigger Piece of Blue

The name is Creighton Bliss. I'm comfortable with dust and practical as gravel. And here I am, sneaking up on seventy, still making a go of the filbert business with my wife, Ella. Still driving up and down this same damn stretch of gravel road in a dirty old pickup truck that barely wants to run. Protecting what's mine with nothing more than a stick.

My older brother and me learned how to fight with sticks from our daddy, who was maybe the meanest cocksucker in all of Oregon. But he had common sense, too. Daddy told us that men of humble means have to make do. So we grew up knowing how to take care of ourselves by keeping our sticks somewhere handy. Take a man down to his knees, I can. In nothing flat. And he don't even see it coming, because he thinks it's some sort of damn joke.

The stick I've got now is barely two feet long. But Lord, I can do some real damage with it. It fits perfectly in the palm of my hand, so it won't slip. Carved it from a limb that fell off my big Douglas fir, out on the slough side of the orchard. Put a little bulge on one end here, for grip and balance. Then I put a point on the other end, for gouging. And then every few months, I rub it down with linseed oil, to keep it from getting brittle. Day in and day out, my stick and me get it done around this orchard.

My mother had me heading for bigger things when I was young. School was important to her. And she figured she'd raise me and my brother Victor up for a better kind of life, especially after our daddy up and took off. But Victor got himself killed when he was seventeen. Happened on a summer job doing highway construction up on the Pass. Apprentice powder monkey. Something went wrong with the charge he was shoving down a hole they'd drilled in the rock. Damn thing blew too soon. And that was the end of my big brother and the plans our mother had for him.

Mother put her hooks into me pretty good after that. Had me doing extra schoolwork. Thinking about college. And she was forever correcting my grammar, so that I'd always make a good impression. But for all her efforts, my mother was not the woman who made the biggest impression on me. She lost out to Ella.

It was four summers after Victor died, and I was supposed to be heading off to the university. The summer of 1950. I had a job moving irrigation pipe up in Mission Bottom. One warm evening I missed my ride home and had to walk back to town. I saw a narrow backroad that looked like it might be a short-cut and took a gamble. Turns out, it took me in a direction I didn't expect.

I was walking down the road by this *very* filbert orchard when out of the wall of leaves steps the most fascinating female I'd ever seen. It was Ella. I said hello to her before my common sense kicked in. I might've even smiled a little; a pretty big deal when you consider that I was all of eighteen, and Ella was older. A grown woman, in fact. The likes of which I had no business talking to that way. But I'll be damned if she didn't get completely under my skin right from the start. She was just standing by the side of the road, wearing that blue dress, her red hair blazing out of the shadows, her easy green eyes watching my every step, as if she liked the way I moved. As if she'd decided to trust me right then and there.

One thing was for sure; I developed a habit of missing my ride home that summer.

I'd see her as often as not, which was enough to keep me coming by. She'd show up in pretty much the same place, looking and acting pretty much the same, except for the time she actually spoke to me. I wasn't quite ready for that. And it was only then that I realized how *much* older she was—at least 15 years. I didn't care because, as odd as it sounds, she seemed younger than me, on account of her being on the slow side. Real sweet, but slow.

Anyway, I'd set my sights on her, and she'd done the same on me, and there was just forward motion after that. Right up to the day I had to meet Boston, who was her daddy.

Ella had walked me up from the road and into their barnyard. Boston came out of his tractor shed with blood streaming down his chin. He'd been hit square in the mouth by a piece of hydraulic equipment that got stuck and then came loose all of a sudden. He carried one of his own teeth in his hand. So when Ella introduced us with her shy and airy little voice, I stuck my hand out to shake his and old Boston just started laughing at me. It was a fearsome laugh—loud and bloody and completely oblivious to pain.

And then he said to Ella, "Sweetheart, who's this sorry lookin' pup of a man who followed you home?"

"Papa, I want you to meet Creighton Bliss," said Ella. "He's from town, but he likes our filbert orchards, so Mama says that makes him okay."

"Okay for what?"

"Mama says he's okay for me," said Ella.

"Hmm," said Boston, taking a measure of me and the situation. "So your mama knows all about your Mr. Bliss, here?"

"Yes, Papa."

"And you think we should trust your mama's judgment on this?"

"She trusts *my* judgment, Papa."

"Uh-huh," said Boston through his bloody teeth. "Sounds like a conspiracy to me."

"What's that, Papa?"

"Well, sweetheart. That's usually my cue to get back to whatever it was I was doing before."

"Before what, Papa?"

"It doesn't matter, sweetheart. It just doesn't matter," said Boston, who then turned his attention to me.

"You ever call filberts 'hazelnuts,' son?"

"No, sir," I said.

"Okay then," said Boston as he turned back toward the tractor shed.

I knew Boston didn't care for me, but I was willing to take my chances with him on account of his daughter. Things kind of went that way for the rest of the summer: me and innocent Ella, meeting up on the road in the evenings; me and suspicious Boston, looking at each other kind of funny from across the barnyard and then across the supper table; me and Ella's clear-eyed mother, Cindy, learning that we could laugh together about Boston's ways so long as he didn't catch us at it. And then, something happened that caught us all off guard. Something bad.

It was after the summer, during the filbert harvest. My irrigation job was over by then, and I was still planning on college. But I kept taking walks out along the road beside Boston's filberts. So I was out there late one afternoon, and I heard a commotion back in the orchard where they'd already picked up the nuts. Back beyond where I could see, where the canopy is dense as hell, and sounds bounce off the tree trunks in crazy directions. It was a confusing echo of something. It set the hair on the back of my neck on end.

Instinctively, I grabbed a stick. I walked straight back from the road, lifting my feet cleanly off the ground to avoid making noise, hunkering down for a better view, trying to get a sense of the trouble. I stopped to listen.

The sound came again, only it was different now. Less of an alert and more of a response. Like something, whatever it was, went from prey to victim. Like a rabbit, maybe. Caught in the teeth of a predator. Wounded, maybe. Knowing it was about to die, no way to escape, no energy to fight, all out fear taking over. Shrieking between final breaths and desperate to live. Drenched by another critter's saliva, licked by another critter's tongue.

Finally, I saw something off through the trees. Something blue. Which made me think it was a jay scrounging for nuts, but it was too big for that. Then I thought it looked something like a peacock's blue neck, but that didn't make any sense, not out in the orchards. Plus, the blue wasn't moving.

Weird thing was, that sound was not coming directly from the blue thing I was watching. It came from further back, off to the right a bit. My stick still firmly in hand, I began moving toward the blue.

That's when I started getting the feeling that I really didn't need to go looking for trouble. That if I just went on about my business, if I just went back to the road to look for my Ella, nobody would know the wiser. But no. I was Creighton Bliss, son of the strong-willed Mrs. Bliss, brother of the late Victor Bliss, heir to the throne of the Kingdom of Bliss. I was responsible for righting my daddy's wrongs. I had no choice.

The damn sound changed again. It got weaker, so even as I got closer, it got tougher to track. I moved from tree to tree, still bending low, trying to hold my breath so as not to make a sound. But my heart pounded up my throat and out my mouth, making a fleshy click that pissed me off.

And then, something moved in the distance. A shape. Dark and angular. Far down the row, too far for me to tell what it was. Some sort of tall animal, I thought. Something that didn't fit.

I moved toward the movement, which brought me right up to that patch of blue I'd seen.

It was a piece of cloth. And it looked exactly like the blue dress Ella was wearing the first time I ever saw her. A shredded piece of blue, not much bigger than a ribbon. Ripped from a bigger piece of blue.

I swallowed hard, bracing myself.

My feet took me toward the trouble. My right hand gripped my temporary fighting stick. My bones and muscles moved me like a cat through the trunks and limbs and leaves. And then, my eyes showed me what I didn't want to see.

Ella.

On the ground at the base of a tree. Eyes wide open and breathing in little bursts. Bloodied. Shaking. Naked except for the part of her blue dress that was held tight to her belly by a sash.

I knelt down to her and looked hard into her eyes, trying to get a read. I was afraid to touch her. But it was only after I finally put my hand on her shoulder that she looked straight at me.

Neither of us could talk.

I couldn't think.

A limb snapped in the distance, still in the filberts. A heavy foot on brittle wood. We both heard it. We both looked in the direction of the sound. We looked back at each other, still speechless. And then, with a quick but unmistakable movement of her eyes, Ella told me to go get him.

My head put it all together as I stalked through the filberts. A stranger had crept into the orchard as Ella wandered out there to meet me. She was watching and waiting for me. And because a childhood fever left her with a very simple view of the world, she was not wary or worried or on guard. She hadn't sensed the danger.

He came at her from out of the blackness of the orchard, quick and strong. He wrapped her up and dragged her way the hell back from the road. Out of sight. Deep back where the harvesters had already been, where no one would go for a long damn time. Back where there was no help for her. Back where it's safe to be bad.

Something moved. That dark shape again. A man, making for the road. He thought he was alone except for the woman he left lying on the dirt. But I had his tracks now. I had his trail. All he had was the need to stop and take a piss just three trees short of the daylight at the edge of the orchard. He was just standing there, one hand on his hip, at peace with his piss. But my fightin' stick changed all that.

One good whack put him face down in his own wetness.

I dragged him back into the blackness, and tied him tight to the base of a tree with my belt. Got him flat on his belly, with the crook of his neck hard to the tree, and his arms reaching around to the other side and then up just enough to keep his elbows from getting traction on the ground. Then I went back to my Ella, whose eyes confirmed that I'd done well so far.

I carried her back to the barnyard, covering her as best I could. Boston froze up when he saw us coming in, so he wasn't much help. Cindy kept her wits about her and tended to her broken daughter, thanking me with her eyes and understanding from mine that the day's work wasn't over.

I headed back out into the filberts, stopping by the outbuildings to pick up a folding pruning saw and a shovel.

When I got back to him, the look in his eyes told me he didn't see me as a threat, even though I had him but good. That was the first time I ever got the feeling that people should never underestimate me or what I'm capable of. That given the right motivation, us Blisses can be a problem. Can't say it was a good feeling, but it was a real feeling. And a lot of times, that's all a person's really got to work with. Real feelings and proper tools.

I took him as far back into the orchard as I could, and ended up at a place where the filberts come up against a brushy slough. About five trees in from the slough, there's this ancient Douglas fir, growing right up out of the filberts. Had to be four feet through the middle, and I couldn't see up through the canopy to figure how tall it was. But height didn't matter, because this man was headed for the depths. And I figured that fir tree to be more than enough marker for a man such as him.

My stick knocked him cold again, and then it knocked him dead.

The shovel dug the holes I needed.

As for the pruning saw, well, I'm just glad it was sharp.

Weeks passed before things started to seem normal with Ella's family. And even then, Boston never really made it back from wherever it was he went in his head when he first saw me carrying his naked daughter into the barnyard. Ella herself got stronger over time, seeming less and less like a victim. And Cindy, she pretty much took charge of the family and the orchard operation.

She made it clear right away that she wanted me to stay on. Said she knew Boston was done for. Because even though he'd made a life out of holding his own, he couldn't prevent what had happened to his daughter, and that fact was destroying him. Said she was mighty angry with her husband about that, because he'd become weak and useless. Said she needed me to help make sure things got done. Especially the hard things.

"Guess the secret's out now," Cindy said to me. "Ella's father ain't half as tough as he always made out. But I can see you're a different breed of cat."

Took my time thinking it over, knowing my mother would be bitter. Spent a lot of time in the orchard, trying to play it out in my head. How I'd forget college. How I'd marry up with Ella, the older woman with an uncomplicated view of the world. How in time, according to what Cindy spelled out for me, I'd have this whole filbert operation to myself.

It wasn't what anybody had had in mind up to that point. But that didn't make it a bad idea, just a new one. Besides which, my world was already changed for good no matter what.

I mean for christsake, Creighton Bliss killed a man, and there was no going back from that. No way of undoing it. In fact, it started becoming clear to me that the only thing I could do was proceed in such a way as to make sure the killing always has meaning. Over the long haul, I mean. Taking that bastard was the first step in a lifelong commitment to my Ella. Didn't know it at the time, of course, but the orchard helped me get it right in my head.

Make it right for Ella, the trees told me. Stay near her. Protect her better than Boston had. Be hers. And if it means changing who you were setting out to be, well, that's just how it has to be.

Ella's eighty-five now. Her life has gotten even simpler. Her world has gotten smaller and smaller. Even though we've got this big ol' place to look after, she pretty much sticks to three rooms in the house: The bedroom, the bathroom and the kitchen, which is where we've always spent most of our time anyways.

I know what people say about my Ella. I've heard them talking about her when they thought I was out of earshot, in places like the feed store and the post office. They say she isn't all there. They say she's a little off. But what the hell do they know?

The way I see it, we're all a little off. And the trick is figuring out how to carry on despite our peculiarities. That's what my Ella's done all these years. I won't go so far as to claim that she actually figured it out, but I do give her credit. I mean, she knew she was going to need someone like Creighton Bliss, the stick fighter. She knew to keep coming down by the road every day that summer so's we could get acquainted. She knew enough to trust me when it really counted.

Yet Ella has no idea what *actually* became of that man in the orchard. And it's been a long time since she's had to wonder what I'm really capable of. It's best that way.

All I know for sure is this: I'm mostly my father's son, and I'm hell with a stick.

Night Paving

Things went fine for the first few hours. Motorists did what they were supposed to do, following the lead of a sun that was supposed to set to the sound of homeward-bound crows, and a moon that was supposed to rise in silence. Midnight approached on the highway, prompting Elsie Bly to think about that American cheese and mayonnaise sandwich inside her father's immaculate black lunch bucket, how soft and comforting it would be, how she would take her time with it, washing each bite down with hot coffee, and then studying the sandwich to decide the location of the next satisfying bite. These little rituals kept her company in the absence of men who'd left.

Anonymity was better pay than money for Elsie, a thick-fingered man of a woman so unburdened by charm that most people avoided her out of subtle discomfort. Nobody doubted she'd be a good flagger. One look said she was the sort who handled the tough things in life with no more effort than it took to bite that sandwich.

The boss on the night paving crew knew what he had in Elsie. He understood all he needed to about her; that things had not gone well, that whatever ate at her was unlikely to surface on the job, that her bearing would intimidate motorists into compliance.

"She'll scare the hell out of people," he told his foreman on Elsie's first night. "They'll do what they're told."

Some people head for Alaska when they get to be like Elsie. They scrape together what they need, leave behind most of what they have, and disappear. She thought about it, too. But Elsie chose to stay where she was, mustering only the will to leave her weathered rental house in Madras just as other Oregonians headed home. Going against the grain of the workday suited her; it extended her solitude.

Four weeks on the job brought changes for the better. Standing alone amid the orange cones and flashing yellow lights of a night paving operation, she started to feel that even if life was not quite worth living, neither was it quite worth dying for. Elsie started looking forward to things: the vibrancy of warm summer nights, the acrid scent of hot asphalt, the squawk of the radios, the heat coming up through her boots, the diesel ballet of heavy equipment, even the semi-benevolent act of guiding strangers through the road work.

She even stopped fantasizing about her own death at the hands of a driver too drunk to understand the stop sign in her hand. The idea had played like a B-movie in her head for weeks before she filled out the job application. How she would stand there in her orange safety vest and bare arms, righteous in her cause, facing down the approaching headlights, counting on the flags and cones and signs to protect her, giving every motorist the benefit of the doubt about their ability to see and understand and respond to all the warnings. Then, how the story would read in the next day's newspaper, making people wonder over their morning coffee about the woman who died out there on the highway, what her story was, who she left behind, who was crying for her.

The fantasy made Elsie feel like a fraud. She was angry with herself for letting it linger as long as it had; she never sought such sympathy in the wake of actual events. *Don't be such a big pussy*, she scolded herself. *Don't be goin' all soft on me.*

Besides, no one would cry. She was as certain of this as she was of August meteors at midnight. There was only the long-ago man with a disturbing posture and twin bags beneath his eyes that raced one another to see which could succumb first to the pull of gravity and the weight of sadness. Those eyes were similar to her own, she had to admit. Elsie called him Frank because it had been decades since he seemed worthy of the name Dad. And Frank the retired dairy farmer, she knew, would not grieve. He'd used up his emotions when his wife—Elsie's mother—died of pancreatic cancer when Elsie was twelve. Frank was useless after that.

For Elsie it amounted to a nasty sack of old troubles, stashed in the back of a forgotten closet.

She was six weeks on the job when the new trouble arrived. The crew set up on a long, straight stretch of highway that crossed the Warm Springs Indian Reservation. A good thirteen miles of two-lane road through open range and high desert, reduced by orange cones to one lane and, when Elsie and the other flaggers decided it, reduced even further. To a full stop.

Elsie tried hard that particular night not to think about how little companionship she had known over the last nine years, since the day Ollie Bly left for good. She'd married him on a careless dare and settled in Reno, where they ran a janitorial service together; twitching, staccato-talking Ollie and lumbering, straight-haired Elsie. They did not have children because she could not bear the thought. Instead they had a date night on Thursdays, always a family-style dinner at Louis' Basque Corner, and always picon punches for dessert that Louis made himself. They had it okay, she thought, and the life worked well enough. The rhythm felt fine.

But there was no rhythm to Ollie's leaving. Everything just came to a halt, the same way Elsie stopped traffic so the pilot car could usher through travelers going the opposite direction. The difference was, there were no orange signs along the way to warn Elsie of what lay ahead. She had not seen it coming. She wished Ollie had just died suddenly instead, because at least that would not have been a decision to leave. Being a widow would have been better. Less humiliating.

Remembering how she had gone after him made Elsie feel ill. She hated how pathetic she became; begging and pleading to keep the life she knew and the man she mostly loved, following him first to Winnemucca, and then to Elko. She believed nobody else would ever have her, and that Ollie was her only shot, so she had to do whatever was necessary. She believed nobody would come to her aid. There would be nobody to console her, to hold her when she cried, telling her to breathe. There were no friends. No family, save for Frank, who didn't count.

Neither he nor Elsie cared enough about the other to bother.

Elsie pushed back thoughts of Frank and Ollie and the rest of it, and returned to thoughts of that pending sandwich and coffee. It occurred to her that she needed to pee and so checked her Timex as a single blue Pontiac idled by her stop sign.

Elsie typically never cared whether the traffic was heavy or light. But this time her bladder had an opinion. Once she released the Pontiac, she planned to slip off into the darkness to dampen a patch of the reservation. Then it would be sandwich time.

A new set of headlights approached in the distance that changed Elsie's plans. Those headlights sparkled and shifted and bounced and spiraled though the high desert night. Then orange running lights came into view up high—a truck. Then came the harmonics of eighteen tires rolling over coarse pavement yet to be resurfaced. And then the wind-rush of air fighting its way around the contours of the cab, merging with the high-pitched whine of the diesel engine doing as instructed.

Elsie's ears listened for the downshift of gears, the gurgle of the jake brake, and the deep rumble of massive kinetic energy slowing to a stop. But this was not about Elsie or what she wanted.

This was about an 80,000-pound tractor-trailer rig landing its bright, broad front bumper on the shimmering red taillights of an idling Pontiac. This was about the sudden transfer of energy from one body in motion to another body at rest, and about the otherworldly way the Pontiac and the truck moved together as one, right past Elsie without touching her, coming to rest in the distant roadside junipers—suddenly silent, save for the hiss of steam, the confused creaking of newly reshaped metal parts, and the sorrowful sound of a stranger dying.

This was also about ice cream, disgorged from the back of the trailer as it flopped onto its side with its rear doors open. Orange Creamsicles. Nutty Buddies. Ice cream sandwiches. Sidewalk Sundaes. Dixie Cups. Fudgesicles. Popsicles. Eskimo Pies. Every kind of ice cream Elsie ever knew. All of it, spread out like flowers in a meadow, giving new dimension to the dark pavement, as helpless as Elsie herself.

The police questioned Elsie until dawn and then sent her home, where there was no ice cream in the freezer. She did not work for a week and a half while grim-faced insurance investigators in short-sleeved shirts poured over the details of the accident, ultimately determining that she had done nothing wrong and clearing her to return to that same ugly stretch of road.

It was not easy going back. Then again, Elsie realized, it was not nearly as hard as losing Ollie or breaking free of her nine-year hiatus from the world beyond her squeaky front door. She knew she could do it, and so did her boss.

"We don't pay 'em enough to stand there and watch someone die like that," said the boss to his foreman on the night paving resumed. "Most flaggers woulda taken a job at McDonald's before trying this again."

Elsie was three weeks back on the job when she finally stopped feeling jumpy about oncoming traffic. She started trusting the eyesight, common sense and brakes of motorists again. And for reasons she could not explain, her weight was down by enough pounds to finally make a difference in how she looked. She chalked it up to the universe trying to make it up to her for having to see what she saw that night with the ice cream and the dead guy. *Like that's gonna help* she thought to herself.

One night, toward the end of the shift, what little traffic there was made the transition from late-night stragglers to early birds. Elsie's belly was long since satisfied by mayonnaise and cheese and black coffee. Her legs, hips and lower back ached from standing but the pain was not intolerable. Her thoughts turned toward the clean sheets she had put on her bed before leaving for work, how nice they would feel after she showered the job off and slipped naked beneath the covers, her hair still damp and her body just tired enough to insure a few hours of unconscious relief from life. This was as hopeful as she ever got.

She had no cars waiting, but three vehicles approached from the opposite direction. The lights set up all around the paving machine illuminated each vehicle as they drew near; a rusty, white Ford pickup, a green VW van from the Summer of Love, and a bronze Buick.

She saw the anonymous shapes of people inside, but did not wonder about who they were or where they might be headed. She only wanted them to move on without incident, each a notch of accomplishment on that night's belt, each getting Elsie that much closer to where she was most at peace—behind her own locked door, where her work boots sit unlaced and empty until they are needed again, and where small routines like brushing her teeth and doing crosswords in ink substituted for a life of consequence.

The bronze Buick fell off the pace and rolled to a stop right beside Elsie, whose impatience surged at the prospect of having to do anything more than stand there, at having to talk when she was least inclined.

The passenger's side window opened an inch at the top, paused, and then dropped all the way down with an electronic glide. Elsie waited, opting not to bend down and look in. Moments passed. Then, a shock of dark gray hair leaned into view from behind the steering wheel. Aspects of a face moved into the strobbing yellow lights. Discolored teeth smiled out. Then an older man's thready voice:

"I've come for you, Elsie. It's time I explained myself if you'll let me."

Those words, and the suddenly familiar face of her father, froze her in place on the pavement.

Red Skirt Escapes

Jenna rose with abrupt grace from the small, close crush of café tables that was the gathering place for her tennis friends. She was one of them, part of the ten o'clock Tuesday morning ritual. One of the stylish young wives who met each week to make their court shoes squeak at the athletic club, but who were much more interested in the noise that came afterward—coffee and diversion at the Hyperion on William Street.

The cacophony of their corner made them all seem the same. But as she rose to full height, Jenna's distinctions showed. She was a true athlete, for one thing. Tall and fit. With muscle definition in her arms and legs worth coveting. And the look of nimble agility suggestive of a life in sports, or a tomboy childhood.

She didn't mean to stand just then. It was a motor response to a thought pounding to the forefront. She wasn't participating anyway, and the other women barely noticed as she rose. Her red tennis skirt was shoulder height to the woman sitting nearest, who turned just in time to face buttocks she herself could never possess. A sneer twitched across Envy's face.

Standing there as if alerted to danger, Jenna was urgent and beautiful. A taut antelope on the Savannah. Braced to leap. Electrified by instinct and luminous in her stance.

Tan shoulders gave her white top an idyllic glow. Her fresh-scrubbed face framed crisp blue eyes and purposeful lips.

Jenna was the effortless blonde her *friends* longed to be.

But they could not see what was going on inside her, and Jenna was forbidden to tell anyone how unhappy she was. How ungratifying it was to live the life she chose. How aimless she felt in the architectural wonder of her house. How empty she felt in the company of her golden boy husband.

It's hard, she realized, to criticize a man who seemed perfect. Handsome. Flamboyant. Generous. Loving. And successful, the shrewdest of dealmakers.

Jenna had no audience for her angst or sympathy for her sadness. Instead, she imagined a Greek chorus telling her to appreciate what she had, and to quit complaining about a life for which most people would kill, and a man for whom most women would do just about anything.

These admonishments fell flat. And though doubt and guilt still nipped at her, she increasingly enjoyed a personal momentum born of inner clarity.

The clock had simply run out on self-loathing.

Now she was compelled to shed her husband's control. To reject his indifference. To slip from beneath the weight of his unwelcome urges.

It was time to stop worrying what others might say, and to accept that happiness could not happen in the absence of authenticity.

It was the moment when possibilities outweighed consequences.

Nobody saw how desperately she wanted out of the quiet mess her life had become, or how she lowered herself in the name of status, or how ashamed she was about accepting his squalid prenuptial terms: STAY MARRIED TO ME FOR AT LEAST SEVEN YEARS...BE EVER MINDFUL OF HOW YOU REFLECT ON ME...NEVER TELL A SOUL WHAT YOU AGREED TO...DO AS I SAY AND YOU'RE WEALTHY FOR LIFE...FAIL ME IN THIS AND I KEEP EVERYTHING...

All anybody saw was how gifted and successful he was, how good she looked, and how much they had.

To be seen so inaccurately, Jenna realized, was the fiercest form of solitary confinement known to woman. There was no compassion flowing to her from the outside. There was no concern for the well-being of her soul. There were no advocates for her rights or advisors for her lines of recourse. There was only that same sad face looking back from the mirror.

The protracted irony of her imprisonment was this: the face in the mirror was both prisoner and jailer. And the ordeal of one coming to terms with the other had already consumed years of her life. Yet Jenna knew the secret to making those lost years actually count for something: make the years ahead exceptionally vital, and full.

Tennis on Tuesdays wasn't going to get it done. Being one of the wives was an embarrassment. It was privilege without honor, and therefore hollow. A weekly charade of shame played out on the red brick sidewalks of Fredericksburg; as good a place as any, she figured, for a woman to find conviction.

Jenna Red Skirt had no plan in place. But an idea struck as she stood there among the tennis ladies. Go ask the advice of the one woman you admire, she thought. Go ask Eleanor Roosevelt what to do next. Just excuse yourself and then slip out the back-door. Get in your car and drive to Alexandria, to the church where Eleanor once sat with Churchill and FDR. Sit with Eleanor in Washington's pew and ask her advice. Be earnest, and maybe she'll look past your hackneyed outfit.

"My God," whispered Jenna to no one. "What an idiotic idea."

"Getting a refill?" asked Envy, lifting her empty cup.

"No," said Jenna as she discarded the Eleanor option and zeroed in on a more direct plan. "Think I've had quite enough."

And with that, she went home to pack all of her other colors of clothing.

All New Dancers

She unfurled from a shallow sleep to the scent of bacon on the stove. Her back hurt from another night on the couch, making Celia feel older than her twenty-three years. It was the consequence—she realized amid the dream-evaporating gravity of morning—of relying on others while she made her way away from yet another love, leaving another boyfriend behind to decipher what had gone wrong.

Celia called the shots in her life, except where cigarettes were concerned. Cigarettes and bacon. Beyond that she acknowledged no weakness.

The decision to get up came easy. Not so, the choice between that first drag of the day and that first taste of bacon. The indecision froze her there, two bare feet on the braided oval rug belonging to the woman known only as Trifle, a hand on each bent and naked knee, her bottom sinking low in cushions that had long since lost their ability to properly support any anatomy.

"Oh my God," she said with an unreliable morning voice that crackled like the bacon cooking in the next room. "My goddamn back..."

"You hungry, darlin'?" asked Trifle from the kitchen in a borrowed Southern tongue.

Celia used Trifle's question as motivation to stand in favor of bacon, causing her right knee to pop in the process. She stretched toward the ceiling, catching her reflection in the ornate antique mirror across the living room. It was floor length. And capable of snaring every victim of vanity who passed.

There it is, she thought to herself as she posed in her t-shirt and panties. *Sure as hell got the legs for it.* A shaft of rare Seattle sunlight shot through the stained glass window on the east side of Trifle's gothic living room, illuminating a billion bits of airborne dust on its way to Celia's legs. It was key light. It showcased her finest physical asset, as if summoned to corroborate Trifle's persistent and persuasive contention that Celia should become an exotic dancer. At least until she came up with a better way to make money.

"That bacon in there?" Celia asked in a clearer room-to-room voice.

"Oh yeah!" came the enthusiastic reply. "Hoppin' and a poppin'."

Celia made her way into the kitchen, dragging her calluses over Trifle's black-and-white checkerboard linoleum floor. Trifle stood at the gas range in a bright, floral kimono-style robe, tied tight at her waist and just grazing that same checkerboard. Celia leaned one hip against the counter and swooned at the scent.

"Mmmmmm."

"Almost ready, child," said Trifle without looking up from the action on the stovetop. "You grab us a couple of plates and I'll get the toast. No eggs today, darlin'. We're all out."

"My dad always says eggs make the world go 'round," said Celia as she went to the lower cupboard where Trifle kept her everyday dishes. "But I think they're over-rated and he's full of crap, like he is about most things."

Celia's harsh words made Trifle look toward her houseguest, her eyebrows arching as if to meter the degree of Celia's paternal resentments. She saw Celia bending at the waist to get the plates, legs straight, muscles taught.

"That's one of the classic moves right there, child. I'm tellin' ya, you're a natural if ever there was one."

Celia stood up holding two green plates. She looked directly into Trifle's eyes and then gave a little shoulder shrug.

"I know, I know," said Trifle. "I heard what you said before. Dancing naked in front of a bunch of horny, lonely men isn't something you ever thought you'd do."

Celia confirmed Trifle's take with a quick glance as she landed the plates on the white wooden table by the window overlooking Trifle's garden.

"All I'm saying," continued Trifle, "is that if you ever managed to get the idea right in your head, you've definitely got the body that'd make those poor saps pull out their money."

"Uh huh," countered Celia. "Their money and what else?"

"Mercy, you judge men so harshly. Why most of them are perfect gentlemen. Most of them are afraid to be anything but gentlemen, 'cause they've got too much to lose by causing trouble."

"Ah ha, you see? You said it yourself," said Celia as she sat in a chair and squeaked it up to the table. "Trouble."

Trifle came to the table with hot bacon nested on paper towels on a plate, opting to rest the topic for the moment.

Though her sixtieth birthday approached, Trifle retained most of the attributes that made her a one-time star among New Orleans' strippers. An *I Love Lucy* shade of red hair. Firm, clear skin that never needed sun to be appealing. Pronounced cheekbones, though her face was never thin. Relentlessly red, full lips. Exotic green eyes—large, welcoming, translucent—*her* ace in the hole.

The sheer kimono robe hinted at the figure she used to have. But Trifle had come to terms with this particular clarity: Even though her body was no longer flattered by the bright lights of the main stage, it didn't mean she still couldn't take money from those men. That's when she moved home to Seattle and opened her own place. The Akimbo Club.

"Lithesome," said Trifle between bacon crunches. "That's how I'd describe your look, honey. The way you move when you walk. The graceful way your shoulders sway and your arms flow. The way your long, blonde hair frames your face and neck, and then trails down your back. I'm tellin' ya, lithesome is a look men like."

"Hmm," answered Celia, her own mouth full of buttered toast.

"And those legs of yours," continued Trifle as she lifted her teacup from the table. "To say they're anything less than a blessing would be a sin. I know you know it's true."

"Well, I do get a lot of compliments. Always have, I guess."

"See?" encouraged Trifle. "And you've got the derriere to go with 'em."

Celia smiled an admission of that additional truth, allowing herself to entertain the idea of dancing, acknowledging to herself that she'd better do something about money, because she was down to her last twenty, and was literally smoking her way through that.

"I'm out of options." said Celia, sipping tea.

"It happens," offered Trifle.

"I mean, I can't go back to Robert. I can't stomach the thought of going back to school, even if I had the money. And there's no way in hell I'd ever go home and ask my dad for help. Uh-uh. No way."

"So," said Trifle as she prepared to land a last little nudge of logic. "What've you got to lose by coming down to the club this afternoon and give it a look? You don't like it, that's that. If you do, then maybe you'll consider it. Either way, darlin', you've got a place here with me while you figure things out."

Celia's face showed resignation.

"More bacon?" asked Trifle, sensing victory.

At four-thirty that day Celia got her first look at The Akimbo Club. It was a pink building on Denny

Boulevard, just below Queen Anne Hill. Fleshy pink. Wedged between a 76 station and a carwash with a rotating elephant on the roof. Perched in a way that was impossible to miss even during rush hour traffic.

Passing cars lifted tire-tread mists to blend with the exhaust and cacophony of another dreary Seattle afternoon in March. *The Great Gray City*, Celia thought to herself as she approached.

An unfriendly feeling settled in on her. She felt the city's indifference to her money problems. Her tendency to bolt whenever the situation she'd gotten herself into became unacceptable. Her underlying high-wire act; that infinitesimal weight shifting between loathing her father for his judgments yet wanting his approval. *Don't be a cliché*, she always admonished herself. *Don't be one of THOSE grown-up daughters.*

But she was. As surely as she craved cigarettes and bacon.

Celia decided to watch the outside of the club from across the street in a Metro bus shelter, where she could get a sense of who came and went. She wouldn't look out of place there on the glass-shrouded bench. She also wouldn't get any wetter.

Celia sat and watched with her legs crossed. She smoked. She tried to look like someone who waits for the bus every day, looking off into nothingness, seeming to ignore the forgettable details of Denny Boulevard on a humdrum day.

Her heart drummed inside, though. Quickened by the thought of walking into the place. Threatened by the knowledge that once inside, her uncertainties would be revealed, her trepidation would be on full display, her down-to-the-bone discomfort would be naked to the world. These feelings, Celia knew, ran contrary to her own rules about always being the one with options, and about never surrendering decisions regarding what was best for Celia.

There it was spelled out in pink neon on the roof: The Akimbo Club. It glowed against the gray of the day. Glowed without blinking, and without apology.

Another, less impressive, sign sat atop a tall metal pole in the pavement just in front of the building. It was white, backlit plastic with blocky red letters that were misaligned but legible. It read "Parking In Rear."

Celia took those words in the worst possible way, thinking of a sexual act for those who'd grown bored with doing it the regular way. The words bothered her, and then she felt bothered by herself for fixing on such a crass interpretation.

The front door opened. A young woman in a man's goose down parka emerged carrying a cardboard box and a long stick. Her bare legs looked disproportionately small because the parka was so big on her. She wore luminous blue stilettos.

Parka girl plopped the box at the base of the white plastic sign. She extended the stick up to the blocky red letters and began removing them, one by one, using a suction cup at the end of the stick. Soon the sign said nothing, a relief to Celia.

Then parka girl began placing black letters up in the air. The first word she created had three letters. A-L-L. The next word also had three letters. N-E-W. The last word had seven. D-A-N-C-E-R-S.

A Metro bus pulled up to the shelter, replacing Celia's view with the smiling close-up of a local, cookie-cutter news team on a bus-side ad. She thought the two anchors looked evangelical, the weatherman clownish. The sports guy looked like the kind who'd frequent the Akimbo Club, causing Celia to gather her coat at the collar. *Smarmy*, she thought. The bus roared off as if it understood, as if it felt duty-bound to remove the sports guy's lecherous sneer.

Again, Celia felt relief. But she also felt disappointed that parka girl had gone back inside. She'd envisioned a conversation between them. A heart-to-heart about what it was *really like* in there.

Not that she didn't take Trifle at her word. She did. But Celia knew her host was decades removed from her own moment of decision, about whether or not to dance naked in front of strangers. Celia wanted a more relevant, more urgent perspective. She wanted to hear it straight.

Another Metro bus pulled up to block Celia's view, only this one had no news teams to menace her. Just a nerdy guy in black plastic glasses who works for Verizon. Celia figured that smug look on his face had less to do with Verizon's cellular service and more to do with the fat paycheck he must get every time they used his mug.

The bus doors opened. Celia watched as the black driver stood, put on a gray sweater, grabbed a cobalt blue lunchbox, and stepped down onto the street. The bus was then empty but still running.

Celia couldn't tell the driver's gender even though just a few feet separated them, and she tried not to stare. But Celia wondered fiercely. The driver took a position a few feet from the shelter and began smoking with determination in the light rain. The bus idled intently.

Distracted as she was, Celia was slow to notice the second bus driver approaching on foot. A short, pale man wearing a Greek fisherman's hat. Beneath his rain slicker, he wore the same gray sweater as the black driver. His lunch was in a brown bag. His stainless steel Thermos rode under his arm.

The new driver let out a birdlike whistle, causing the black driver to spin in his direction, the cigarette in a mid-drag glow. Celia caught a glimpse of femininity in the black driver's spin move, and concluded that ovaries were present and accounted for.

The two drivers made an odd pair. The taller black woman gestured dramatically with her cigarette as she spoke, the shorter pale man listened, shuffling his carried items as he struggled to scratch behind his right ear. Celia couldn't make out their conversation over the rumble of the bus. But she noticed that when the black driver stopped talking to take another puff, the white driver said something funny, because the black driver failed to fully inhale her smoke before she bent over in a sudden fit of laughter, which Celia heard distinctly.

The white driver checked his wristwatch, then gestured with his entire head in the direction of the impatient bus. The black driver lifted her chin abruptly as a good-bye.

He got onboard, adjusted the seat to his liking, and drove away.

Across the street, two construction workers entered the windowless club, their workday done. Their body language suggested a boyish excitement. They had parked in back.

The black driver sauntered into Celia's direct view, passing in front to take a seat on the bench. Three or four minutes passed. Celia shifted her position, not because she was uncomfortable or needed to create distance between them, but because she couldn't help it. She glanced at her Timex even though the time was irrelevant. An overweight businessman darted from behind the Akimbo Club and then inside. Finally, the driver broke the noisy silence.

"Makes a body wonder what happened to all the old ones."

"What's that?" asked Celia with a furtive glance.

"The old dancers," replied the driver. "Sign don't say what became of the old dancers. Just that they got some new ones."

"Huh," said Celia, appreciating the insight but not wanting a conversation about it.

"No sir," continued the driver. "Ain't nobody gonna go round asking about the ones that got too old. Or the ones that got fat. Or strung out. Uh-uh."

Celia listened while watching her own feet, her own tired-looking checkered Vans. They instantly reminded her of Trifle's kitchen floor, and the idea of look-alike shoes and floors made her chuckle under her breath.

"You think it's funny do ya?" said the driver. "You think the old dancers ain't worth wondering about?"

"No," said Celia as she made first eye contact with the driver. "I was thinking about something else. Sorry."

"Ain't no skin off my back," said the driver, her body language showing no hint of offense. "I'm just sayin', makes a body feel kinda sad for the ones that got turned out. What'd they do when they couldn't do that job across the street no more. That's all."

It occurred to Celia as she sat there in the bus shelter with a big decision to make about whether to dance or not, she had a second decision to make as well; whether or not to engage the driver in a deeper conversation. The second one suddenly looked more attractive than the first one.

"Whadaya figure?" asked Celia as she angled her knees and Vans in the driver's direction. "About the ones who used to work there, I mean."

"Ain't no way of knowin' for sure."

"Guess not. But I get the impression that maybe you had a thought on the subject."

"Well," said the driver as she also repostured her body for conversation. "I suppose I do."

"And?"

"And I'm thinkin' the best way to put it is that they're like one a them Roman candles, you know? The colorful fire goes in all directions. Some up. Some down. Some sideways. Thing is, sooner or later, they all burn up and disappear. Like they was never there in the first place."

Celia took a moment to play with the image planted in her head by the driver. The sparks and the smoke and the sound. The temporary satisfactions of fireworks in general. But then a new question came to mind.

"What about dignity?"

"Dignity?! Ha!" exclaimed the driver as she rolled her eyes toward the gray skies.

"What I mean," continued Celia, "Is that I wonder whether any of the old dancers ever managed to leave with their dignity still intact. You know? When their dancing days were done."

The driver brought her gaze back to the street, to the shelter, directly to Celia.

"What's your name, young miss?"

"Celia."

"Well, Miss Celia. I seen a lot on these streets since I first got to sweet ol' Seattle. Seen a lotta places like this here pink thing across the way. Seen a lotta comin's and goin's. And I seen a lotta goin's on, if you know what I mean."

Celia pursed her lips to indicate she understood.

"Okay then," continued the driver. "The thing is, most of what I know in this ol' life is probably wrong. But I'm pretty sure I'm right about one thing."

Celia's eyebrows lifted.

"Any woman who takes up strippin' for a livin', well, she's probably a little low on dignity to begin with. She probably had something happen to her along the way that made strippin' seem like it ain't so bad. Or maybe she done made some bad decisions, whatever. Point is, a woman can't leave with something she didn't go in with. A body would do well to remember there's a big difference between being down on your luck and down on your dignity. BIG difference."

Celia's smooth forehead frowned as she absorbed the driver's wisdom. And as she did, yet another Metro bus pulled up in front of the shelter. The forward door opened to reveal the broad grin of a robust-looking black man behind the wheel.

"That there's my man," said Celia's benchmate. "Time for this one to get on home."

She stood up and moved away from Celia, stopping at the first step to look back. Her thin but now elegant face revealed there was more to say.

"There's a lot more mileage in being an almost-stripper than being an ex-stripper. Trust me, Miss Celia. I know."

The bus door slapped shut, sealing off the last flow of a stranger's insight. The bus took off like a giant stage prop exiting right, restoring her view of the Akimbo Club and leaving Celia alone again to consider her decision.

She checked her pocket for cigarettes and felt only an empty package. She felt hungry. The tip of her nose felt cold, which reminded her of nakedness. She thought about how the line between good and bad can blur in a hurry when you're alone in a city as gray as Seattle.

Next morning, Celia awoke on Trifle's couch. Her back hurt like the day before. But there was no sunshine streaming in this time, nor was there bacon cooking. The house felt chilly, prompting Celia to pull on her hoody and jeans before barefooting into the kitchen.

She found Trifle at the table sipping tea. The only light came from outside, but there was enough to see that her host was off to a rocky start; no make-up this time, nothing done to correct the effects of pillows on hair. Celia found a cup and the hot water. The tiny earthen jug containing tea bags clinked in a way that made Trifle turn her head toward the noise.

"Mornin', darlin'," said Trifle in a small voice.

Celia nodded her reply as she sat opposite the older woman, whose expression suggested disappointment. Steam danced in the air between them.

"When did it happen?" ask Celia.

"When did what happen?"

"Whatever it was that made it possible for you to take up stripping."

"Exotic dancing," corrected Trifle. "Show business."

"I'm not sure it matters what you call it," said Celia. "You're still in the business of taking off your clothes in front of strangers."

"They're not all strangers," said Trifle with a territorial tone. "At least not any more."

Celia looked straight into Trifle's eyes, measuring the likelihood of an honest answer and coming up short. Then she looked away, zipped her hoody up to the neck, adjusted herself in the chair, and bobbed her tea bag as her next thought formed up.

"I can't do it."

"I know."

"I thought maybe I could, and I feel bad because you've been so nice to me, and you opened your door to me."

"But?"

"I couldn't even make myself go in. And you wanna know what stopped me?"

Trifle grimaced a yes.

"I realized every girl in there has a dad, or at least had one. And more importantly, I have a dad."

"Darlin', I think that's what they call a blinding glimpse of the obvious," said Trifle with unexpected sarcasm. "Everyone comes from someone."

"Uh huh. And in my case, that someone is a man named Frank Freeman of Valparaiso, Indiana. A quarry worker. A Presbyterian. A father to four girls, of which I'm the youngest and most difficult."

"And you figure Frank Freeman of Valparaiso wouldn't approve."

"He'd do more than not approve. He'd be ashamed, and hurt, and there'd never be anything I could say or do to fix it. And even if enough time passed for his shame and pain to let up, he'd still go to his grave wondering what became of his youngest daughter's dignity."

"And you just couldn't do that to him."

"No, I couldn't. I can't. I won't."

"Well there it is, darlin'. Decision made. Time to move on to whatever's next for you. Time to make room on Trifle's couch for someone else."

"I'll get my things together this morning. Be out of your hair as quick as I can."

Celia stood with her tea, pausing just long enough to see that Trifle's eyes did not rise to meet hers, and then turned to walk away from that black-and-white moment in that black-and-white kitchen. When Celia reached the doorway to the living room, Trifle spoke again.

"I was raped when I was thirteen. The boy next door. Nobody believed me. Nobody did anything."

The news held Celia in the doorway. She turned back toward Trifle, who continued to look to the spot where Celia had sat. Celia leaned a shoulder into the doorframe, sensing Trifle's need to say more, waiting. Then it came.

"Got it right in my head a long time ago," proclaimed Trifle. "Used to bother me, now it doesn't."

Celia waited.

"Everything that ever happened to me..." continued Trifle. "It's what made me the woman I am today."

Three minutes later Celia stooped over her beige suitcase, packing it. The posture hurt. But she took comfort in realizing this truth; a backache was evidence of backbone.

Slugger

Blood drips from Wheeler's nose.

"Only way to stop it is to hold your head back," says a woman wearing the University of Oregon's green and yellow.

"Put your index finger right here," says a man's voice passing behind Wheeler's hunching frame. "Like Hitler's mustache."

Wheeler raises his right hand in a thank-you wave, acknowledging the advice without looking up from the sight of dark red drops disappearing into the stagnant water. He realizes he should have seen this coming, and should have expected nothing less from her. He remembers that where the unconventional Amanda Park is concerned, he should never be surprised by anything she does, drunk or sober. Not even something as bizarre as this.

Wheeler keeps his grimacing face away and down, avoiding the onlookers. But it's halftime of a rivalry football game between the University of Oregon and the University of Washington, and thousands of people are milling about, too many of them clustered right around Wheeler: some sober, some drunk, some stoned, several curious about the man hanging his head over the rail of the footbridge, dripping blood into the motionless creek outside the stadium.

He dislikes being a sideshow to the gray-skied game they'd all been watching, this boyish, beleaguered man who wears his heart on his sleeve, and who'd had vodka for lunch. But anonymity and middle-age wisdom keep him from feeling embarrassed.

"Okay. All right. I'm not totally screwed," Wheeler mutters as he straightens his stance, absent-mindedly making the Hitler finger and scanning the crowd for Amanda. *Where'd she go?* he thinks to himself. *Tall girls with limps are easy to spot.*

He steps up onto the lower rail of the footbridge for a better view. He'd acquired the stepping up habit as a short kid, and had kept it into adulthood out of necessity. Now a youthful fifty-two-old restaurateur, Wheeler typically serves up a smirk at life's every wrinkle, even the unpleasant ones. He knows that sooner or later, he'll make a story out of it that'll make others laugh, or at least feel better for a while.

People like Wheeler. But he's too wise, too nonchalant to analyze the reasons why. His practiced indifference, however, does not extend to Amanda. He aches to break through her emotional fortress. He campaigns to understand her pain.

Maybe she made it back to the bookmobile, he thinks as he snakes his way through the crowd, which instantly ignores him as he falls into the flow. It strikes him how easy it is to blend in, and how very little effort it takes to stand out. *Remember that for happy hour.*

Wheeler sees the faded baby blue bookmobile off in the distance, back behind the legions of luxury cars and SUVs that dominate the gravel parking lot, back against the cottonwood trees that retain only the heartiest of their summer leaves. She bought the bus-like beast to tour the homes listed with Amanda Park Realty, but so far it's only served as a contrarian tailgater.

He breaks free of the green and yellow masses and pushes back through the parking lot, crunching his trail boots into the gravel, negotiating row after row of cars with the grace of a young O.J. evading would-be tacklers, thinking hard about what he'll say to her next, because what he said last earned him a bloody nose.

Thirty yards from the rusting bookmobile, Wheeler holds up. His nose no longer bleeds, but he feels dried blood around his nostrils and works to clean it away. He feels his ruddy three-day beard and wonders whether it wouldn't have been better to shave clean, as if Amanda might have found him, and more importantly his words, more acceptable. *Dumb ass. You think she's that simple?!* Wheeler extends the fingers of both hands up beneath his round wire rim glasses to massage his brown, bloodshot eyes, buying time, trying to find the words, the wisdom. He sweats beneath his black fleece pullover. He unzips the front and scratches the base of his throat, unconsciously twisting a tuft of chest hair. *Wing it, Wheeler.*

He pops around the front of the bookmobile and bounds up the steps, looking as though nothing is wrong. Friends are assembled for halftime drinks amid the shopworn maple bookshelves, each person nursing a plastic cup of team spirit. They're discussing why it is they all drink so much. And then, with his resonate and bellicose voice…

"Where's the head librarian? Hey! Anybody seen Amanda?"

Of the eleven aging alumni pressed together in sloppy cacophony, not one heard the question. So Wheeler comes up closely behind the largest man in the group—a congenial and drunken fifty-year-old who goes by Houseboy, owing to his former college job as a sorority dishwasher. Wheeler puts his knee into the back of Houseboy's knee, causing the bigger man to buckle a bit. With Houseboy's ear instantly closer to the linoleum floor of the bookmobile, Wheeler leans in and whispers a repeat of the question.

"Haven't seen her since you two took off at the start of the second quarter."

"Okay, man. Thanks."

"Hey," says Houseboy, finally turning to look directly at Wheeler and blasting him with vodka breath that rivals his own. "You no looky so good."

"Oh hell, Houseboy. I look gorgeous today, just like every day. And you, my inebriated friend, are clearly in no position to pass judgment on appearances."

"Go to hell," Houseboy says with a rubbery grin.

"Yeah, yeah. I'll get there soon enough. First I gotta find Amanda."

"Pretty damn tough to lose a six-footer with a fake leg, man. Check under the Jumbotron?"

Wheeler exits the bookmobile and heads back into the masses, appreciating that Houseboy remembered Amanda's affection for the giant video scoreboard, and then questioning why a woman who'd overcome losing her leg in a car wreck couldn't handle things better than this.

He ascends the zigzag ramp up the side of the massive berm that retains the concrete of college football. Once at the top, he notices weather coming. Rain again. A broad gray band of new clouds, lighter at the top and darker at the bottom, dragging itself along the too-green terrain. Probably fifteen minutes off, but coming his way with a conviction he'd hoped to see from Amanda.

He wonders about his sense of timing as he navigates toward the Jumbotron. He questions his decision to speak up when he did, but he has no doubts about what he said to her, because for him the truth always holds sway, even over bad timing.

Wheeler finally sees Amanda in her pink dress near one of the massive uprights holding the Jumbotron. She poses the way a proper drunk contemplates breakers on the beach, faced into the wind. Bold but at ease. Arms crossed in front. Feet set apart at shoulder width. Chin held high enough for the tendons in her perfect neck to show. Her stylish brown hair is moving but still frames her stoic face, her powerful brown eyes, her story arc eyebrows. She pretends not to notice Wheeler.

Strangers to her expression, that look of frail defiance, stand no chance of comprehending the woman or the moment. Both are complex, forbidding, even intimidating. Wheeler sees through it, though. Wheeler knows how this goes, how Amanda gets so bound up by her own rules and disciplines that she sacrifices her own best interests, how she willingly forgoes happiness, how stubbornness rules beyond reason.

He moves nearer—gently, respectfully—understanding his credibility evaporates if he pushes too hard at the wrong moment. He'd already pushed hard once today. This moment beneath the Jumbotron, Wheeler knows, warrants something else: a patient hand extended toward the nose of a skittish cat, offering a friendly scent, letting the animal move nearer on its own terms, leaving the decision to the one who is afraid.

She says nothing.

A gust of wind nudges both of them, causing Wheeler to turn and face the stadium, standing beside Amanda between the elephantine legs of the Jumbotron. This wind carries a thousand scents, each scoured from the belly of the stadium, each lifted from the person or thing the wind collided with before it swept up the unpadded stands behind the end zone, up to where all eyes go when real play on the field is instantly reinforced by the video replay. This television screen was so large, the future of two people can play out beneath it, Lilliputian-style. Wheeler considers the irony of it as his eyes water in the wind: This conflict between them is happening in full view of an entire football stadium, yet they are invisible.

He begins.

"You're reminding me of your dad right now. That picture you have of him in your office. Standing up on Hurricane Ridge, looking out into nothing."

"He loved it up there. Loved the Olympic Mountains."

"You miss him, don't you."

"Every damn day. But you wanna know why I'm missing him today?" Wheeler glances toward her and lifts one eyebrow in the affirmative. "It's because he's the one who told me it's okay if the things I do don't always make sense. He's the only one, Wheeler."

"Including what you did today?"

"Oh yeah. Especially what I did today."

Not too bad, Wheeler thinks to himself as his first attempt at recuperative conversation comes to a natural close. He gazes straight ahead, just like her. He glances aside with caution, monitoring her. The teams retake the field below, and the stadium reabsorbs the thousands of fans who'd left their seats at halftime to further complicate the day for Wheeler and Amanda. The resurgence of crowd kinetics is palpable, and Wheeler reads it as his next opportunity for progress.

"Know what I like about you, Amanda Park?"

"Huh" she answers without conviction.

"I like that you treat Duck football games like the Kentucky Derby. I like that you always wear a dress, when the world around you thinks it's okay to just show up in whatever."

"Why be like everyone else?"

"Exactly my point. You're pretty much the opposite of everyone else. I love that about you."

"Thanks," she says with a somewhat softer tone.

"I also love how brave you are."

A few moments pass as Amanda considers his last comment with arms crossed tight beneath her breasts. She reaches down to the midway point of her right thigh and taps three times on the prosthetic leg beneath her dress, signaling that she knows all too well what Wheeler means. Though the tapping is dull and muffled, the sound explodes at Wheeler. This not-so-secret secret of hers, this fake leg attached to an authentic beauty, this struggle of hers to keep the loss of a natural leg from becoming the focal point of her existence, this rigid way of living that keeps everyone at arm's length—even those who are closest—making her unknowable.

And then, Wheeler lets out a chuckle. His stubbled face expands into a broad grin, which Amanda senses without seeing.

"What?" she says with irritation.

"You."

"Explain, please."

Wheeler doesn't explain. He turns away from her a bit, looking up into the press box, and then up into the billows of the gray clouds overhead. He shakes his head gently from side to side, still grinning.

"C'mon, Wheeler. What's so damned amusing?"

Wheeler turns back to face Amanda, seizing his opportunity.

"Well, you know, I'm just thinking about that poor kid with the sousaphone."

"He'll be okay."

"Are you kidding me? That guy's gonna be in therapy for years.

"He'll be fine."

"The poor son-of-a-bitch, just walking along with his band camp buddies to the stadium. And there you are, waiting at the footbridge."

"I hate the Huskies."

"You reach up under your dress and unhook your leg."

"I especially hate the Husky marching band, and those damned purple uniforms."

"You're leaning on the bridge railing to keep your balance."

"I coulda done it standing on one leg if I wanted to. That's how much I hate those arrogant dogs."

Wheeler breaks into laughter, unable to speak for a moment. "There you are, holding your leg like a honey baked ham, taunting those poor kids in the clarinet section. And then the saxophones."

"And then the trumpets," she interrupts. "And then the trombones. I was there. The drunk chick brandishing a plastic leg. It's a wonder they didn't arrest me."

A drop of rain lands on Wheeler's forehead, alerting him that the second half has begun beneath them, and that he and Amanda are sobering up. The clouds hang low. The afternoon darkens, triggering the field lights. For a moment Wheeler imagines himself in an old Steve McQueen movie, attempting to escape from a prisoner of war camp, causing the Nazi searchlights to come on. Then it occurs to him that he is a prisoner, and that Amanda is his aloof captor.

"So why the sousaphone player?"

"I dunno."

"Poor, pimple-faced fat kid."

"That big-ass sousaphone just pissed me off, okay? And then, when I saw the fat kid with that goofy Husky grin on his face, and all the brass hugging him in a way I'm sure his mother never did, I just had to do something about it."

"That's pure horse shit, my dear. "

"No it isn't!"

"Right." says Wheeler with whipass sarcasm. "So, you take your own leg by the ankle and just fuckin' clobber the kid in the back of the head…all because the mere sight of him pissed you off? "

She doesn't answer.

"Hey, I was there to witness the whole thing…displaced aggression, or transference, or whatever the hell they call it. And I got the bloody nose to prove it."

"I didn't mean to hit you, too."

"All I know is, you've got a helluva back swing."

"The more important issue is sousaphones should be outlawed, plain and simple. Ban them completely. The most offensive musical instrument ever conceived. Too big. Too excessive. Too bright. And with a damn ridiculous name."

"Even if all that's true," observes Wheeler, "what you did was more than a little weird. Maybe even a little perverse. And I'm not sure even your dad woulda let this one go."

"If you think I'm so perverse, where do you get off saying what you said to me a while ago?"

"That's just how it works with me, Slugger."

Rain. It drifts over the stadium from the west and is nearly upon them. It falls at a languid angle, dragging the cloud bottoms down to the ground, to the parking lot and the synthetic turf, blurring the lines between earth and sky, an orderly smear of partially-erased pencil lead gray. Wheeler understands the weather seeks to help him, and he accepts the offer. Resolve and conviction dominate his face. Droplets dot his glasses. Clarity fills his eyes. He turns to her again, causing Amanda to lower her gaze and her chin. Their eyes lock. Her eyes ask *Are we really going to finish this now? Right here*? His eyes do not blink, which is her answer. She, in response, launches a look of exasperation toward the clouds. Then she's back in Wheeler's eyes.

"Mack Wheeler."

The mention of his father puzzles Amanda and alters her expression.

"Stay with me now," he coaxes. "Mack Wheeler died on June 14, 1998. It was a sunny morning. I'd been there at the house since the night before to help mom, because we knew..."

"It's my duty as head librarian to point out that you're committing a serious non-sequitor here. In the frickin' rain, no less." Her diversionary comment fails.

"Mom and I were sitting at the kitchen table about nine or so that evening. Just sitting there with the one light directly over us. Dad's over in the living room in a rented hospital bed, propped up, dozing in the shadows. We're talking about something that happened when I was a kid. Something funny. So we're laughing a little bit."

"You ne-e-ever laugh just a little bit."

"So I guess my laugh woke Dad up, because I look over there, and I can see him grinning. Then I see him raise his right hand and give me a little wave. The way a small child might wave good-bye. It was sweet as hell."

"And you waved back?"

"I did. And I'm lucky I even noticed him over there, because that was the last time my dad and I ever communicated. That was it."

"Hmm."

"A few minutes later and he's asleep. Only he never wakes up again. And all through the night his breathing kept getting noisier and noisier—that croupy, gurgling sound from deep down inside. The hospice lady had told us to expect it.

"The next morning he's more peaceful. So peaceful it makes me feel comfortable enough to take a walk up the hill behind the house, to clear my head and stretch my legs. It was just a beautiful morning. Bright and promising, you know? I almost forgot why I was there. It was a fantastic feeling. I never felt so alive…"

The expression on Amanda's face softens as she listens, forgetting herself.

"I wanted to stay up there. I wanted to stay in that mood, but I headed back down to the house because I knew Mom was afraid. Just as I opened the back door, Mom called my name. I could tell something was up. She sounded like a little girl. She sounded small. And when I got to the living room, I saw her standing at the foot of his bed, frozen."

"Your dad."

"His eyes were open, but empty. Not looking at anything, or anyone. He was gasping for air. He was fighting it. But what the doctor told us was right: that sooner or later, that kind of cancer catches up to people."

"What'd you do?"

"Sat on the bed beside him. Wrapped him up in my arms. Held onto him so he'd know he wasn't alone, so maybe he'd be less afraid on his way out…"

Now the rain makes a statement in the stadium. Ponchos and umbrellas replace the crowd behind Wheeler, who can only hunch up his shoulders in response to the downpour. He holds his gaze on Amanda, whose dress now clings to her contours in a darker shade of pink. She is visibly chilled.

"Mortality, Amanda. That's what my dad reminded me about on June 14, 1998. I don't give a crap if it sounds cliché, but we only get so much time here. Only so much time to get it right. To do what's right."

"Right," she says without really understanding.

"Goddamnit, Amanda. You're what's right. We're what's right. And we don't have much time!"

She raises her chin and her gaze back up in a complete return to defiance in its purest form. And just then, the crowd roars its approval for a play on the field, but she takes it for her own. Seeing this, Wheeler stops cold. He reconsiders. He puts the palms of his hands up in the air and rain between them, fingers spread wide to halt the conversation.

"You don't wanna get it. You know what else? If you don't have the balls to do what's right for yourself, then maybe I've been making a big-ass mistake all along."

"Maybe you have."

He looks away from her, toward a horizon that doesn't exist on rainy days in Oregon. His lips tighten. His brain convinces his heart to give it up for now.

"I hear vodka calling my name," says Wheeler with spiteful resignation. "See ya in the bookmobile, and feel free to take your time."

"There's a fresh Absolut in non-fiction."

He starts to leave her beneath the Jumbotron, his hands in his pockets, his head down. But after a few steps he spins back toward Amanda, and uses his busy-kitchen voice that everyone can hear. "YOU THINK YOU'RE A CRIPPLE…"

He stops mid-sentence, takes a beat, then marches right back to Amanda. Then, in a more intimate voice:

"You think you're a cripple because of your leg. But at the risk of being melodramatic, I'd say it's your heart that walks with a limp."

He turns and leaves.

Had he stayed mere moments longer, Wheeler would have seen his final insight eviscerate Amanda's resolve, because those words could just as easily have come from her own father's mouth—and this unsteadies her to the bone.

But Wheeler, he sees none of it.

Virginia with the Miata

She showed up at the tire store last Tuesday. I hid in the back office to avoid that sickening conversation about what we've both been up to, and so I wouldn't have to tolerate her judgment over the fact that I'm no longer a professional photographer—that I'm a guy who wears a white, short-sleeved work shirt with *Walt* embroidered in red thread over my heart.

Oh how the mighty have fallen, I imagined her saying. Or maybe not even that. Maybe I dreaded nothing more than that look of hers. That expression. The one she thought would make us both famous...

My boss, he shot me a look that questioned why I was taking my lunch early that day, without first getting his okay. But Tom was cool. He knew something was up with me, and that I had my reasons for hunkering down with my egg salad sandwich. We've all got our reasons. We all take our turn hanging back so as not to be seen by that certain someone out front, not wanting to face something from our past. That's just how it works in the tire business, because everything and everyone tends to come full circle—pun intended.

Tom said part of the reason he hired me was because I looked a little like Radar O'Reilly from M*A*S*H. He said I could learn all I needed to know about tires in due time, but that it'd be good for business if people became a little intrigued about the famous-looking face behind the counter. They'd say something to me, he figured. They'd want to talk. And to Tom, talking was selling.

I already knew plenty about tires. They were my weird little obsession long before I began pretending photography was my thing. It was a long time before I trusted Virginia enough to tell her about tires and me. When I finally did, a good eighteen months after we became a couple, she got that look on her face.

Whenever those icy, indifferent eyes were aimed at me, I was diminished. The color brown was never so cruel. But, whenever they targeted my four-by-five camera, and then got reinterpreted by my lens, I felt safe. The lens offered immunity: it took what good Virginia had to offer and left the rest invisible.

I always had this bizarre sense with Virginia that we were on the clock, right from the time we met at one of my first showings. As if we were only allotted a certain amount of time together to get it right, whatever *it* was. There was an urgency between us that was like a lit fuse, burning up the atmosphere in a way that created more of a suction than an attraction, slamming us into one another, each of us asking in our own way, "What's in it for me?"

For me it was two things, and neither was love.

Hell, maybe it was really only one thing. Maybe it was just about my career behind the camera. Maybe it was what I perceived as the ambient light of being with a woman like Virginia, photographing her. There was a kind of credibility wrapped up in all of that, I suppose. The kind I wouldn't know more than once in my life. The kind I probably never deserved, but I chose not to stew over that.

At first I was irritated that a visitor to my show was attracting more interest than the work on the walls. Virginia had an exotic quality about her that made my black-and-white prints on the walls seem ordinary. She moved with a grace and patience that made all other visitors seem insincere; pausing as she did before each print—not so much looking at the images as deciphering them—judging them one by one and then revealing her judgment with tiny head movements up and down or side to side. This caused her thick, straight, bobbed hair to shift slightly, each dark strand functioning as a needle on a gauge, measuring.

I watched from across the room as she worked her way around, her silent critique troubling me less and less. I held my spot and waited, striking my best hands-together newsman pose, planning my first words. She stepped within a few feet of me, looking at a print I was particularly proud of—a portrait of a hazelnut grower titled "Creighton Bliss." As she moved toward the next print, I spoke:

"He had a big ego for an old guy who grew nuts," I said in tone that assumed we'd spoken before.

Virginia stopped right in front of me, landing her eyes in mine, waiting for more.

"He kept telling me what a good fighter he was, and how he could drop me to my knees before I knew what happened."

"Huh," she finally said, understanding I was the photographer. "That's why you shot him then? Big ego?"

"The lens loves big egos," I said. "The bigger the better. Fills the frame like no other subject."

"Was the old man full of it?"

"He was full of himself, and that's all I really cared about."

That last part was a lie. Because the thing that always bugged me about photography was that there were too many things you had to care about. But I was trying to appear as if I'd reduced my craft to a singular focus, as if I'd already mastered everything else. Virginia bought it.

"Do you think ego is a bad thing?" I asked, hoping she'd linger a few minutes longer, thinking how hip we must look together, standing there in the bright gallery lighting, having such an artful conversation.

"Ego's got its place," she said, crossing her toned arms. "But then, so do grace, humility and generosity. Don't you think?"

"I suppose," I replied with half grin. "A person can afford to be graceful and humble and generous about whatever it is they're offering the world, so long as the quality of their work warrants it."

"What exactly do you mean?"

"Excellence in whatever we pursue, whatever art we do, is the catalyst for good things to happen. Excellence shifts energies and vaporizes barriers, and when people encounter excellence in a setting like this, for example, it changes the way they see the world, if only for a while."

"Uh-huh," Virginia said as if she understood.

"It changes the way they see the artist, too. But take my word: excellence can't happen in the absence of ego."

"So ego is good."

"Ego is great. Couldn't do without it, but it gets a bad rap," I said as I leaned in and shifted to a whisper. "So we'd better just keep this between you and me. Tricks of the trade and all."

"Got it," she said with a wink. "So then, it must take a lot of ego to do something like nude photography, right? Just to show the human form without any hint of a snicker, I mean. Without a sexual connotation."

I was thrilled to the core that I got to discuss anything sexual with Virginia there under the bright lights, but I kept it mature. "On the part of the photographer or the model?" I asked.

"Both."

"The answer is yes. But it's not so much about the model being confident enough to take it all off, or the photographer being bold enough to show the resulting images to close relatives."

"No?"

"No, the ego part of nude photography is more about being dead certain that the model and photographer don't conspire to create some sort of breathless, over-heated cliché." As I said this, it occurred to me that I was on quite a roll with my little speech, so I continued. “The tricky thing about nudes is that there’s a three way tug-o-war going on between art, erotica and pornography. And the ego, well, it’s what makes sure art is the winner.”

“You’ve given this some thought, haven’t you?” she said with a trace of admiration.

“Some.”

“But have you ever put your ego to the test? Or are you more a man of theory than practice?”

My egg salad sandwich didn’t last long enough to keep me out of harm’s way. I even managed to get a little on the front of my shirt. Virginia sat in the waiting area near the popcorn machine. Her head was down in a fashion magazine when I darted from the office to the men’s room; her position was unchanged when I came out. I slipped past the waiting area to the job board out in the shop, to see what she was having done. A free rotation on her Miata, the white one I’d helped her buy just before we split. I hated that car.

I liked it at first because of the way she looked in it with the top down, wearing those big sunglasses of hers, going about her business with a little more style than the average woman. It made me proud to say she was mine, as if Virginia could be possessed.

Hell, the irony of it was, she possessed me.

The first time I photographed her was also the first time we made love, right there in my studio. She called it being in the moment, and I didn't exactly resist. It wasn't long before she started teasing me by calling me her horn-dog photographer, which eventually morphed into her calling me phodographer. Virginia thought that was really funny every time she said it. I didn't see the humor, but didn't say so until it was too late to matter.

Thank God we never moved in together. That would've made things even worse when the wheels came off. She didn't have to retrieve that much stuff from my place, and I had even less to retrieve from hers. She already had all of the props and wardrobe for the series we did of her. The hats, scarves and dresses. The jewelry. The boots and shoes. All that stuff, and I was glad to see it all go, because it ate at me.

None of the large format black-and-white prints we made ever sold, not a single one. The only place we could ever get anyone to hang them was a second-tier coffeehouse called Cup-a-Mud, a chaotic place with squeaky floors and moody patrons. Still the owners had wall space and a willingness to let Virginia and me hang ourselves, so to speak. Seven pieces from the series went up there, and there they remained for six long months. What an embarrassing half-year that turned out to be—people snickered and pointed and sometimes laughed at the work.

Virginia as Cleopatra with her breasts exposed. Virginia at the foxhunt with her bowler hat and bare breasts. Virginia as a Crusader without a breastplate. Virginia as a fortuneteller with all revealed. Virginia as a Royal Canadian Mountie trying to get her man with her red tunic undone and open. Virginia as Confucius with her wisdom fully shared. And then there was that one with Virginia as a nun with a nasty habit.

I was such a fool, letting her talk me into it. But she was convinced the work had merit. She talked all the time about how in stark black-and-white, her nipples were as dark as her eyes, and that the combination and composition would lift the images to a transcendent level, that people would celebrate the work and want to know more about the creative team that put their heart and soul into the project. She envisioned a touring exhibit that would make its way around the country, from gallery to gallery. She even had a title worked up to go with the artist's statement: *Where Egos Dare*, she called it. Like the famous movie, only with egos in place of eagles. She said it was clever. Brilliant, in fact.

Worse still, we had the audacity to hang a portrait of the two of us in that coffee place, right above the artists' statement where people could see it. "To satisfy people's curiosity," Virginia said. I went along. There was no historical theme and no skin. Just me and Virginia, looking for the world like Gary Burkoff and Parker Posey in a PR shot for a television pilot that never should have been. Eventually I just couldn't handle having it all out there for the world to see. In turn, Virginia couldn't handle my growing jealousy over her willingness to share her breasts with strangers.

"Grow up," she scolded on the day we had it out. "Don't be so small. Don't be so petty. Don't make the human body out to be a bad thing when in fact it's a thing of beauty."

Virginia was right, of course. She often was, but I couldn't help the way I felt, just like she couldn't find a way to interpret my jealousy as an expression of affection.

"Walter!"

She said my name from a good forty feet away, loud enough for everyone to hear, but with a familiarity that made it seem as though we were the only ones in the tire store. She stood, closed her magazine with a slap, rolled it as if to whack a bad dog, and marched right to me at the front counter. It was all Tom's fault, I thought, as Virginia approached. He'd made me get back out there.

"Walter? Is that really you?"

I felt my face muscles form into what passed for a grin, but it was chagrin for sure. Next thing I knew my right hand was extended across the counter, over the advertised specials of the week, to shake her hand, which was cool and bony and dry. Mine was the opposite.

"Aren't you going to say something? Walter?"

Words swirled in my head, but none volunteered for duty. So I just kept shaking her hand until she pulled it back. She flicked her eyebrows up in combination with a slight head jig to demand a response. Impatience blinked like distant lightning in her eyes.

"I was going to say that this is not what it seems," I blurted out. "But the truth is, this is exactly what it seems. So hello, Virginia. Hello. You're looking well."

"There was a rumor going round about you, but I didn't believe it."

"What, about me working at Tom's Tire Town? Listen, Virginia," I said defensively. "Judge ye not."

"No, no, not that. For chrissake, Walter. It's not like you're the first artist to find safe harbor in the trappings of an ordinary life. People do it all the time."

"Whew! Well that's a relief," I said sarcastically. "For a minute there I thought I'd gone off and done something original."

"Oh, Walter."

"It's Walt, now. Like it says here on the shirt."

"WALT!" she said as if belching, prompting me to look at her over my glasses. "Is there someplace we can talk?"

"Not really," I said. "Sorry. Plus which, I just got back from lunch. So, you know..."

"Huh. Well," she said with resignation.

"Yeah," I said with a palms-up gesture that meant this is my reality now, so deal with it.

"Okay."

"Okay," I echoed. "Back to work."

"Back to my magazine, I guess."

Virginia turned and glided away, destined for another fifteen minutes of waiting before her rotation was done. I held my position at the front counter, calling people's names when their cars were ready, taking their money. And all the while the questions nagged at me: what was that rumor going round, and why the hell does Virginia want to talk to me now?

I replayed our exchange in my head, considering whether I'd done myself proud, and how I might have done better. I thought about what a tedious little man I was to waste my time on such unimportant questions, and then I immediately consoled myself with the thought that the great majority of people are tedious and small, and that in fact I fit right in. Forget the pretense of being original. Forget the mystique of being an uncelebrated artist. Go instead for the anonymity of life as a tire guy, beholden to no one except bosses like Tom, and to old ladies who don't quite understand the importance of siping their new tires for better foul weather traction and longer tire life. Nobody knew my story or bothered to ask, and it was a relief. I always felt so self-absorbed before. So fraudulent. Standing there in the gallery, dressed in pompous black, waiting for strangers to ask me about my motivations and techniques, waiting to hold court. Turns out there was no court, but there was a crime or two. For instance, my being so stupid as to let Virginia shanghai my life, and Virginia for being so checked-out as to think people would admire her sophomoric fantasies.

Tom stepped out from the shop and handed me a job slip as he made that moist click-click sound out the side of his mouth, which was his way of saying chop-chop. I took it the way a kid takes a two-dollar bill from a stingy aunt, eager but uncertain. There was no charge, because the customer was female. Retail chivalry, Tom called it.

I shifted my weight so as to steady my belly against the drawer of the cash register. I cleared my throat with my eyes needlessly fixed on the job slip. And then:

"VIRGINIA WITH THE MIATA? YOU'RE ALL SET."

Sometimes I felt like an auctioneer or a revival preacher, using a bigger voice than normal to call customers from the waiting area. Sometimes I felt like a weary waitress at a pancake house on Sunday morning, calling the names of the hungry and impatient listed on a yellow legal pad. This time, with Virginia, I felt like none of those people. This time I just felt like crap.

She approached the counter preoccupied with something in her large purple purse, which she then plopped beside the cash register as if to make some sort of statement about how full and complex her life was since we'd gone our separate ways—or at least that's how I took it. She looked up and into my eyes, which I hoped were delivering a steely gaze but probably weren't.

"Here are your keys," I said, handing her yet another noisy symbol of life since me. "No charge."

"You didn't have to do that, Walter."

"I didn't. The boss figures you'll come back one day when you need a set of tires. He'll get even then."

"That's nice, I guess."

"Yeah, we're all about being nice around here. Ever seen the slogan in our ads? A nice place to buy tires?"

"No."

"We're hell for nice and nobody can claim otherwise."

"Whatever you say, Walter."

"It's what the boss says," I offered by way of quashing any undo credit. "I just do the job. That's all."

We both stood there on opposite sides of the counter for a few more moments, unsure what to say or do next. It flashed through my mind that I should try to explain why I became jealous over those nudes of her we did together, how I grew uncomfortable with strangers seeing her breasts, which made me possessive—for better or worse. But I knew she saw it as for worse, so I said nothing. Why go there again? It hadn't gone well the last time.

"Well?" she finally said as she slung that purple purse over her bony shoulder to leave. "Aren't you curious about that rumor going round among our old friends?"

"The rumor about me?"

"You. Me. Us."

"Nah," I said with a shrug. "Doesn't really matter that much to me what they're saying. Not anymore anyway." I was instantly pleased with myself for tapping into such nonchalance, and that I didn't automatically take the bait as I always had before.

"Huh. Sounds like Walter the Photographer is a little tougher than everyone thinks. Good for you," Virginia said as she reached for a slip of note paper and a pen by the cash register. "No really, I mean it. Good for you. But I'm gonna jot the rumor down for you, just in case you change your mind. Is that okay?"

"Since when do you ask permission for anything, Virginia?"

The question caused her to stutter-stop right in the middle of a pen stroke, but she finished up, folded the note in two, and handed it across the counter. I held the note as if it were slimy or hot or smelly, and then slipped it in my shirt pocket just below my name patch.

"And now it's back to work for you, WALT! I'm off."

Virginia turned from the counter and walked away. Her citrus scent lingered for a moment as she disappeared through the tire store's double glass doors—the harsh scent of new tire rubber retook command soon after. I stood at the cash register a few moments longer than necessary, my arms locked straight to hold my weight against the counter. I looked up at the highest row of tires on the floor-to-ceiling display racks in our showroom, exchanging all of the air in my lungs for a fresh shipment, trying to shift back into the reality of black rubber.

Tom did it for me when he stuck his head and shoulders through the doorway from the shop and held out another job slip.

"Walt, my man!"

I broke my pose and spun around to grab the slip from Tom, read the information, and then turned to my audience near the popcorn machine.

"Chester with the bronze Buick!" I said with my auctioneer voice. "Good to go!"

The pale, old man named Chester was slow to put down his hunting magazine, but in time he stood before me in his all-beige outfit. It made me wonder what age it is that guys like him decide it's okay to wear nothing but beige. I speculated about the reasoning behind that particular palette; my favorite theory being that as some men grow nearer to the end of life, they instinctively begin to dress as if they're as naked as a baby, ultimately ending up as they began. I always wanted to find a way to ask guys like Chester about their clothes, but I never did because I didn't want to embarrass them.

I finished up with Chester. As I watched him waddle toward the same double glass doors that had sent Virginia on her way, I took her note from my pocket, wadded it up and threw it away. Just before Chester put his gnarled hands on the door's push bar, the screech of tires on pavement filled the air—that nauseating sound of bad trouble. Then came the impact: a percussion I could feel in my ribs and belly, metal on metal, deep and destructive. And then came the Tinkerbelle sound of small things landing here and there.

Chester froze at the double doors, staring outside. Every pair of eyes in the showroom was trained on Chester's back, trying to decipher the meaning of the sounds. The first person to overcome the inertia of the moment and reach Chester's side was a younger man wearing a bright Hawaiian shirt.

"Someone call 9-1-1," he shouted. "Have 'em send an ambulance!"

Tom already had the shop phone in his hand, making the call. I ran toward the doors to see for myself.

I did a quick inventory of car colors in the intersection in front of the tire store: a blue Chevy undamaged; a silver Toyota on the sidewalk but undamaged; a champagne Ford SUV sitting in an odd position in the street, with one end higher than the other; and a charcoal gray BMW laying on its side, hissing and leaking.

No white Miata.

The phone by the cash register rang, so I walked back to the last place I would ever see Virginia, uncomfortable in the knowledge that she got away unharmed.

Splendid Purpose

Dinner at the Pierce's house had always turned out well for the Thompsons, a young couple still finding their way and struggling in private to grasp how they might one day have what the Pierces had. Their dinner together on Friday, July 30, 1965, was their last.

Gwen Pierce's day had centered on taking two of her four sons for swimming lessons at the YWCA in Salem, where she sat in the bleachers reading her Bible amid the scent of chlorine and the echoes of instruction. Frank Pierce spent his Friday reading back issues of *Scientific American,* seated at his metal desk in the fluorescent control room of the Bonneville Power Administration substation, which he supervised. Jim Thompson picked up and moved stacks of green veneer with his propane-powered lift truck in the plywood mill that employed him, and where nobody knew he couldn't read. Lilly Thompson had a day filled with laundry and Faulkner and humming original melodies.

Gwen and Lilly had become friends before their husbands had. The two women met in the church choir, which Gwen led and Lilly sometimes accompanied on six-string guitar. They'd both found it easy to talk. When the newlywed Thompsons first started going over to visit the more established Pierces, the women were instantly comfortable. The men were initially reserved but got friendlier over time, despite their distinctions.

The Thompsons entered from the covered breezeway that separated the Pierces' garage from the house. The wooden screen door creaked when Jim opened it for Lilly as they stepped into Gwen's kitchen.

"Lilly! Jim! C'mon in, kids," said Gwen. "I've got meatloaf in the oven, and everything's just perking right along. Lord willing, we won't starve tonight."

"Hi, Gwen," said Lilly.

"Oh how ya doin', sweetie? How was your day? Good, I hope. Get all that laundry done like you said? And oh, did you try that new detergent I was telling you about? The one that comes in the shape of big pills?"

"Oh yes, I found excitement at every turn today," answered Lilly.

"And how are you, Mister Lifttruck?" said Gwen. "I bet you moved a lot of veneer this fine Friday, didn't you. Now tell me something, Jim. Do you keep count of the bundles as you go?"

"Somebody counts 'em," offered Jim.

"Oh?"

"Yeah, I'm pretty busy just trying not to run over anybody."

"Everyone's safe when Jim's driving," said Lilly.

"Oh well, isn't that just the way it oughta be?" said Gwen. "But listen, Frank's out in the garage fiddling with something."

"Yeah?"

"Yes, so why don't you, you know..."

"Go out and play?" said Lilly.

"By the way," said Jim as he moved toward the screen door and the garage. "It was 237 bundles today."

The three wooden steps down into the garage from the breezeway squeaked as Jim entered.

"James, my man. How the fuck are ya?"

"Hey, how's it goin'?"

"Oh, you know. Same ol' shit."

"Yeah?"

"Yeah, looks like we made it to another weekend, though."

"Looks like you got yourself another project goin' there," said Jim as he moved closer to the bramble of colorful electrical wires on Frank's workbench. "'Lectric fence on the blink?"

"No, it's workin' fine. I just wanted to see if I couldn't get a little more juice into the line."

"Animals aren't grasping the concept?"

"Now there's a good way of puttin' it," said Frank as he turned his attention to the device on the bench. "Damn stupid animals anyway. I tried to explain electricity to them. How it flows like water and all. How it flows right through 'em to the ground when they touch it."

"Stupid damn animals."

"Well I tell ya what, we'll smarten the bastards up right quick. Shock the holy livin' shit out of 'em. Just as soon as I back out a few ohms."

"What the hell's an ohm?"

Frank stopped tinkering to look up at Jim, recognizing his opportunity to explain a little science to a neophyte—Frank loved science above all else.

By now the kitchen was bursting with the commotion of Gwen's cooking: she in her apron, slicing potatoes and onions into a sizzling frying pan, Lilly looking for ways to help.

"So how's it going for you kids?" asked Gwen without looking away from her knifework. "Any progress on what we were talking about before? Limping toward the weekend, you called it?"

"Well, sometimes it seems like things are better. Especially after we spend time with you guys."

"Is that so."

"I mean, you two are so good to us. And your home is so wonderful, and your things, and your life, it's all so nice," said Lilly with true appreciation.

"Frank works hard, and the Lord provides."

"And you know what else? Jimmy and I are filled with envy for your view here. That big picture window, and that big green valley down below, and those hilltops across the way. We're both kinda stuck on that."

"That's the good Lord again."

"Sometimes, when I look out there, it just makes me feel like everything's possible, you know? Like I can do anything I set my mind to. Like actual happiness is just waiting out there."

"Well, it's like they say, dear. Inspiration is where you find it."

"I always believed that," said Lilly. "Or thought I did."

"But?"

"But, well, it gets so hard to stay positive, and I don't normally have trouble with that."

"But getting married changed something for you, because it's not what you thought."

"It's embarrassing."

"It's okay. Really. You're not the first young bride to get turned around on her way home from the altar."

Frank's garage was a tidy, disciplined shrine to his life as a narrowly educated, analytical, electrical engineer—one who struggled to suppress a dark side he never spoke of. Schematic drawings decorated the walls. Tools of various kinds seemed to hold their breath, each in its place, dreading the next time Frank drew near—Frank the obsessed scientist now bending down close to the electric fence project, Jim the young intern at his side.

"How in blazes did you ever come to know so much?" asked Jim. "'Cause it makes me feel kinda dumb."

"So you think I know a lot, do ya?"

"Seems so."

"Here, you go ahead and hold this circuit tester on the terminals. We'll check the current."

"And me, I don't know my ass from a hole in the ground."

Frank grunted at the comment to dismiss it.

"How'd we do?" asked Jim.

"Oh yes sir. We got some more juice moving down the line. That oughta zap the crap out of 'em."

Frank shifted his attention back and more fully to Jim.

"And as for what I know, or what you think I know, let's just say that I've always placed a high value on understanding how things work. From a scientific point of view, I mean. My dad, who by the way I do not miss in the least, used to call it the curse of curiosity."

"I never got much science."

"Yep, I figure that if something can't be explained in terms of science, it just isn't worth bothering with."

"Yeah?"

"Yeah. Numbers and equations and the motherfuckin' laws of physics. That's mostly what gets it done for me. I was just drawn to it, like metal to a magnet."

"Great," said Jim in a flat tone.

"And as for you, you crazy cocksucker, you're more like a moth drawn to the flame. You're young, goddamnit. You don't know what you know. So ease up on yourself."

Jim was briefly frozen by Frank's words, staring down at the now complete electric fence project on the bench top. Frank walked across the garage to an aging refrigerator.

"Hey, wanna beer?"

It wasn't particularly warm for a July evening in western Oregon. Gwen decided they would eat at the kitchen dinette just inside the screen door, as if it wasn't summer at all. Fresh air breathed through the screen though. Gwen and Frank's children could be heard out in the breezeway, setting up a card table for their dinner, pretending it was a restaurant. Gwen tossed a green salad as Lilly put plates and flatware on plastic placemats with an amber leaf pattern.

"Would you say Jim's been good to you so far?" inquired Gwen gently.

"Oh, he's been very good to me. Maybe even a little too good."

"Too good?"

"What I mean is, sometimes he's nicer to me than I deserve, because of how I behave."

"Lilly!"

"What?!"

"Have you been testing the poor man? Tell the truth now."

"What do you mean?"

"I think you know what I mean," said Gwen stopping her task. "You've been trying to get a reaction out of him. Trying to make Jim mad, so you can figure out how much silliness he'll tolerate from you. Right?"

"I wouldn't!"

"Oh, but you have. I can see it in your eyes now, as clear as the Big Dipper on a clear night."

"No ma'am."

"Yes, ma'am. And here's how I know, sweetie. You two knew each other how long before you started dating?"

"A week."

"A whole week. And how long after that was it that you two got married? Right after state fair, wasn't it?"

"About three months. But we knew!"

"Of course you knew. That's how good marriages get started. But what you didn't know, and obviously still don't know, is each other."

Lilly went quiet, absorbing Gwen's observation.

"Listen, I've got four sons and no daughters. So you may well be my one and only chance to give advice, woman to woman."

"What."

"Push him around if you must. But only until you find out what you need to know."

"And then?"

"And then, live your life accordingly."

The double garage door opened to the fading light of dusk. Frank and Jim meandered out, each with a beer and the glow of a cigarette. The task lighting on the workbench inside was their backlight. Both men leaned against Gwen's black Galaxy 500.

"You know, sometimes you seem a little envious of what I've got here. And I notice you hardly ever turn down an invitation for Friday night supper."

"Well…"

"Well, nothin'. You really like what you see here. The life. The stuff. And that's okay, man. 'Cause you've got somethin' I really like. So it's kinda equal."

"I don't follow."

"Oh, c'mon, man. You think I haven't noticed that Lilly of yours? She's a fine young thing. And you're a lucky bastard."

Jim felt instantly uncomfortable with the turn of the conversation, and went quiet in response. The silence lasted long enough for both men to pull hard on their smokes, and then their beers.

"All I know for sure," continued Frank with a mild sense of glee. "If I had me a woman like that, I'd sure be hangin' my britches on the bedpost a lot more than I do now."

Jim shifted his stance, taking a moment to consider his next words—how to avoid alienating Frank, whose peculiar friendship he valued despite the older man's coarse behavior.

"Lilly's a good woman, and I'm lucky to have her."

Frank snickered at what he perceived as a double meaning.

"What I mean is....

"I know damn well what you mean."

"You know..."

"Spit it out, man."

"Okay, listen. It's just not something I'm gonna do, okay? I'm not gonna talk about my wife that way. She deserves better."

"And mine does, too. Right, Jimbo?"

The meal was all but on the dinette and nearly ready. Gwen hand-whipped some cream for the strawberry shortcake she'd planned for dessert. Lilly stepped in to set up the electric percolator for the coffee to come afterward. The mood remained confessional.

"So. You two argue very much?" asked Gwen. "'Cause it wouldn't be all that unusual, you know."

"Some, I guess. Mostly as the week wears on."

"Yeah?"

"Yeah. It's like Jim just gets grumpier and grumpier with each day. And then, if his foreman does or says something stupid, look out."

"Hmm. And then Jim comes home mad."

"Mad and sad, Gwen. All at the same time. And just between you and me, it kinda scares me sometimes. Because there we are, sitting in our crummy little roadside rental with broken siding, no money to go do anything, and no way to get past the feeling that maybe we made the mistake of our lives, getting married like we did."

"Ohhh," said Gwen with honest sympathy.

"And the worst of it is, Jim gets so blue. And so far away. Like there's almost nothing I can do or say to bring him back or make him happy. And then I start asking myself, 'Lilly, how'd you manage to get yourself in such a predicament?'"

"And that's when you start feeling sorry for yourself, and you start testing him."

"If you say so. But if it's true, the poor guy doesn't deserve it. Because he's got enough trouble just keeping his own head above water, doing a job he hates, trying to keep us afloat."

"But you can't seem to help it, can you."

"No, I can't."

"Well...."

Lilly waited for Gwen to continue, anticipating a rebuke.

"Okay, forget about Jim for a minute," said Gwen with an even more serious tone. "Let's talk about you."

"Me?"

"Yes, you. What's become of you these last few months? Where'd Lilly go? Where's the girl who taught herself how to play guitar? Where's the girl who sings like a meadowlark? You know, the one who understood that even when things take a turn for the worse, there's reason for optimism. That one. Where'd she go?"

"How do you...?"

"How do I what?" interjected Gwen. "Know so much about the you you used to be?

"Yeah, that."

"Good Lord, child," said Gwen as she once again stopped her work. "Why do you assume yourself to be so anonymous? Like you're invisible or something."

"But I'm nobody, except maybe for being Jim Thompson's wife."

"Ah-ha!"

"Ah-ha, what?"

"That's what we all see. That somewhere along the way to becoming Mrs. Thompson, you maybe lost a little too much of yourself."

"You talk about this with other people? About me?"

"Church people, and very few of them. Only the good ones."

The kitchen grew instantly quiet. From outside Gwen and Lilly heard one of Frank's loud laughs, followed by conversation they couldn't quite make out. Then they heard the children in the backyard.

And then the women heard a nighthawk high above the Pierce's home: that shrill trilling sound they make when diving full speed toward a summer evening insect: peaceful air suddenly warping around angled wings and tight tail feathers, making way for the hungry bird.

"How about you? Ever lose yourself in your marriage to Frank?"

"Apples and oranges."

"That doesn't seem right. I mean, how could we be that different? Our situations."

"You mean besides you being twenty and me being thirty-five with four kids? Well first off, you're you and I'm me. And second, I completely lost myself in the Lord long before I met Frank. Which made it impossible for me to do the same with Frank. You see?"

"Not really."

"Frank's my husband, honey. But God Almighty is the master I'd do anything to please. I mean anything!"

"Well you know, I was baptized when I was nine," countered Lilly. "I know the Lord, too."

"And he loves you for it. But you've gotta understand, there's more to it than that for me. It's more complete. So as much as I love my husband, or even my kids, it's nothing compared to how much I love my Lord. Trust me, you have no idea."

"Wow."

Gwen went to the screen door and called for the men and children to come in, then immediately returned to the stove to get the meatloaf out of the oven. Lilly was still trying to take it all in—the magnitude of Gwen's conviction.

"Mind you, it's not like I'm anything special in the eyes of the Lord. Far from it. It's just how I choose to live my life, okay?"

"Okay."

"Okay!" said Gwen, who leaned in close to Lilly to rest her case. "And you, you've got a choice to make as well, about how to be happy on your own accord. You deserve to be happy."

The screen door blew open with force and banged into the wall of the breezeway. In came Frank and Jim, followed by a blur of faceless boys.

"Damn kids, always in the way," said Frank as an almost-apology for his progeny. "Hi ya, Lil!"

"Hello, Frank. Teaching my Jimmy some new bad habits out there?"

"None that he doesn't want to learn."

"Uh-huh," said Lilly with a hint of suspicion.

"Sit down now," commanded Gwen. "Let's eat."

The sound of forks on plates grew louder and more frequent as the adults ate their way through the meatloaf and fried potatoes and peas and salad. They each drank cool well water from amber-colored tumblers the Pierces had collected by loyally buying their gasoline from the station that gave one tumbler free with each fill-up.

Frank slurped as he drank, which went unacknowledged by Gwen-the-tireless-talker. But Lilly and Jim noticed, and made quick eye contact over it. The plates were swept away by Hurricane Gwen and replaced by strawberry shortcake and whipped cream in mismatched cereal bowls.

A towering electric percolator appeared at the center of the table, silvery and graceful, full of just-brewed coffee, ready to chase away the sweetness and perpetuate the conversation.

"Frank, did you tell Jim about your weather stripping project," prompted Gwen.

"Yes, started telling him out in the garage," said Frank. "About how the house is like a big, breathing animal, with air moving in and out all the time, only you don't need to open doors or windows for that to happen."

"Drafts," added Jim.

"Right," continued Frank. "And nobody takes drafts seriously in this year of our Lord 1965. But they should. Because our people at the BPA say we're gonna run short of electricity one day, even with all of our hydroelectric."

The two women shared a quick glance that signaled their mutual disinterest in Frank's pontifications, so they veered off into a parallel conversation.

"You guys watch Jackie Gleason last Saturday?" asked Lilly.

"We always watch," said Gwen.

"We were going to, but the TV is on the fritz. Again."

"What's gonna happen to our dams," asked Jim on Frank's subject.

"Tell me your favorite part of the program," said Lilly to Gwen.

"Nothing's gonna happen to the dams," said Frank. "But something's gonna happen all around the dams."

"Well, I like the *Honeymooners*, of course," said Gwen. "Except for all the yelling."

"What are you talking about?" pressed Jim. "What's gonna happen?"

"And I like the opening part—the monologue?" said Gwen. "That's always funny."

"People, man. Population. It's gonna explode. Hell, that's something you and Lil oughta know about, right?" said Frank with an evil wink.

"My favorite part is the dancing," said Lilly. "And those big song and dance numbers."

"You mean to say," continued Jim for clarification, "we ain't got enough juice to keep up? Are you kidding? With all that water? All those rivers? All that goddamned rain?"

"All those big flowing skirts," added Gwen.

"And all that kicking and twirling in high heels," said Lilly.

"And all those boys in stretchy pants," continued Gwen.

"Stretchy pants?" grunted Frank to Jim. "For chrissake!"

The men gulped down their last bites of strawberry shortcake, pushed back from the table, topped off their coffees, and drifted into the living room to inspect Frank's weather stripping on the big picture window. The Pierce's view of the valley had been replaced by a black, cloudless nightscape. There were no streetlights outside to fend off the dark.

Gwen and Lilly lagged behind, still enjoying their Gleason tangent, eventually finding their way to the picture window as well.

"3M makes a good product," said Frank. "Stands for Minnesota Mining and Manufacturing."

"Three Ms and one W," said Jim. "For weather stripping."

"Did you know I always wanted to be a June Taylor Dancer?" offered Lilly.

"Nooooo," said Gwen is mock disbelief.

"And sometimes, when no one's around and I'm watching the show, I get up and dance when they dance, like this."

Lilly playfully twirled in her blue summer dress, prompting Gwen to attempt the same move, though with less grace. The men took notice. The theatrics irritated Frank.

"Gwenny, how about you flick on the light so Jim can see what I'm talking about here," commanded Frank.

"You mean so Norton can see, don't you?" said Gwen, referencing the Gleason Show character played by Art Carney.

Lilly grinned at the inside joke as Gwen began to move toward the light switch. But she was stopped short by Jim's suddenly urgent voice.

"What the HELL!?"

"What, Jimmy?" said Lilly.

"Wait, don't turn on the lights," cautioned Jim.

"Whatcha see out there?" probed Frank, now alert as if threatened.

"I honestly don't know what I'm lookin' at. But something tells me this isn't what you'd call normal."

All four were transfixed at the window, each struggling to comprehend what they saw: a brilliant green orb of light, moving left to right across the darkest part of the night sky to the north, traveling at a slower pace than satellites they'd each seen before, seeming to project a faint green ambient light onto their four faces.

"Oh my Lord," said Gwen in fear.

"Son of a bitch!" said Frank in anger.

"Look at that!" said Lilly with wonder.

"I knew something like this was gonna happen someday," said Jim in defeat.

The Day After it Happened

BALL OF FIRE CROSSES SKY; Residents from Portland to Salem reported seeing a "bright green, dinner-plate sized" fireball descending in the north sky at between 10:15 and 10:30 p.m. Friday. One witness here, R.J. Newman, 44, of 2200 SE Crest Dr., a retired Air Force colonel and veteran B-52 pilot, said the fireball was like nothing he had ever seen. "It started as a point of light 45 degrees above the horizon moving steeply earthward at a slight easterly angle. It grew as it fell to the apparent size of a dinner plate, trailing a tail about three times

the diameter of the ball in length. It appeared to extinguish itself before reaching the horizon," he said.
—*The Oregonian*, July 31, 1965

FRANK

Radio static filled every square inch of Frank's home office. The door was closed. Frank sat within whispering distance of the ham radio microphone. His quest to understand what he'd seen through the picture window had grown to a full and haunting consumption.

He had to understand it. He knew there had to be a solidly scientific explanation, and that someone somewhere would have some sort of a mathematical/astrophysical/electromagnetical equation on their chalkboard or in their head that would make this whole unsettling phenomenon make sense. Not knowing was too much. It would not let him rest. It would not let him think about anything or anyone else. A dispassionate man by nature and training, Frank had become passionate about this. He needed an answer that could be interference-fit into his view of the world. He needed to snug his micrometer onto this experience and take a precise measurement of it. He needed to know where to plot this on the table periodic of elements that was his life.

"It's the damnedest thing I ever saw," said Frank into the microphone. "I mean, it just came out of nowhere, right in front of my picture window. Big as life. Bright green and glowing. Over."

"Copy that," said a man's voice over the radio. "Sounds like you saw something crazy. Whadaya make of it? Over."

"That's the thing. I don't know what to make of it. Not even close to understanding it. Couldn't have been a meteor, 'cause they're not green, and they sure as hell don't move that slow. Over."

"Do you think it mighta been, you know, from someplace else? Visitors, maybe? Over."

"Aw, now you're going all Rod Serling on me," scolded Frank. "I never believed in that stuff. In aliens, I mean. Do you? I sure as shit hope not, because that's just useless science fiction, man. Over."

"What about some kind of aircraft? Maybe something totally new, like something that hovers. Over."

"For chrissake, I've read everything there is out there about that shit, and there ain't nothin' that gets more than six inches off the ground. So no. I didn't see some sort of manmade aircraft. I'm sure of it. Over."

"Must be a big deal to you, 'cause it's the only thing you ever want to talk about now," said the man on the radio. "How's everything with the wife and kids? Four of 'em, right? Over."

"Yeah, that's right," said an impatient Frank. "Four kids and a wife. Big deal. I'm gonna sign off now. Over and out."

The next day found Frank awash in the harsh fluorescence and disturbing energy of the substation, seated at his metal desk, hunched over in a deep read, attempting research. He was dying to know which particular law of physics prevailed in this instance.

Not understanding had always been hard on Frank. But this. This incident. This unexplained phenomenon. This got the best of him. Undid him. Broke him down to his most basic parts. Right down to the molecule. To the atom. To the proton and neutron and electron.

Frank was not energized by the quest to understand. He was not able to take charge. Rather, the experience drained him off and left him useless but still burning with the acid of uncertainty.

On this particular Wednesday, in this dead-hearted state, he barely seemed to notice when Gwen walked into the room carrying a brown paper bag and a red plaid Thermos. She stood there a moment, then reached out to bump the paper bag into

Frank's shoulder. He was slow to respond, but eventually turned to give her a look.

It was obvious from Frank's body language and expression that he was irritated at being interrupted. Perhaps it was her mere presence. Yet he resigned himself to the tradition of lunch with Gwen. He pushed back from his desk, forcing Gwen to move back. They walked together, making their way out of the control room and out to the grey concrete steps on the front of the building. They sat on the top step, in sunshine.

Frank and Gwen ate their ham sandwiches in a practiced manner, their years-old routine. Few words passed between them as they took turns sipping hot tomato soup from the plastic lid of the Thermos that doubled as a cup. They sat an arm's length apart, but the distance between them was now far greater and more visceral than ever.

When all that remained was crinkled wax paper, and empty brown bag, and a soup-stained cup, Gwen stood up to leave.

"Next time, bring the paper napkins," said Frank as Gwen stood up to leave. "You forgot 'em today."

Gwen looked over her shoulder at Frank briefly as she walked toward her black Galaxy 500. She got in her car, started up the guttural V-8 engine, backed the car away from the substation's sidewalk and out onto the rural gravel access road, and then drove away with more purpose than normal. Frank remained seated on the steps, watching Gwen disappear in a roiling cloud of late summer dust.

Gwen's kitchen missed her more than did Frank. She'd been gone and out of touch a full week before Frank finally got into any sort of rhythm for fixing meals for the four boys she'd also left behind. It was just past dusk, not unlike the night they saw the green orb in the sky. The only light came from the bare bulb over the kitchen sink. Frank removed five TV dinners from the oven, one by one. He lined the aluminum trays up on the counter in neat order, and then peeled back the foil of each to reveal what the packaging represented as fried chicken, mashed potatoes, corn and apple cobbler.

"C'mon, you guys," yelled Frank with enough volume to reach every Gwenless corner of the house. "It's ready."

The sound of four hungry boys approaching the kitchen offered Frank a moment of familiarity, but that comfort would quickly turn cold. The boys thundered in nonetheless.

"Drink water tonight," ordered Frank. "Or milk. Or whatever you want."

"Are we eating at the table together?" asked the oldest son.

"Sure, if you want," answered Frank. "Or go eat in your rooms. Or in the barn. Hell, you guys can do whatever you damn well please. Left to my own devices, I'm gonna head on out to the garage. Take care of couple of things."

Frank's soulless indifference to his sons was enough to make them all disperse from the kitchen—heads down and confused—with the TV dinners, except the youngest one, who lingered with a question.

"When did you say Mom is coming back?"

"It's like I said, boy. You mother apparently decided she had to go off on a mission. A religious mission. And these things can take a while. You understand that?"

"Uh-huh."

"Alright, then…"

"But do you think she's worried about us, Dad?"

"Well hell, son. She's been gone a week now and I haven't heard a peep. So I guess she's taking it on faith that we're all gonna be fine."

"I guess I get it, but I don't like it."

There is a long silence between father and son, enough time for both to hear a yellowjacket buzzing the light over the sink and then randomly plinking its body in the kitchen window, hoping for an exit. It was time enough, as well, for Frank to flash on this thought: as offensive and disgusting as it was for a mother to ditch her children, he secretly wished he could do the same.

"Can I eat in the garage with you, Dad?"

"No, you better go find your brothers."

Frank found himself back in the kitchen many hours later. The wall clock said it was 4:24 in the morning. Now the only light on was the one over the dinette, where Frank sat alone, surrounded by books and magazines, hunched and focused and mumbling. Catching light on the dark counter behind him, the carcasses of five TV dinners.

Next day at the substation, Frank paced outside in the switchyard. His subordinates watched from a safe distance as he moved erratically among the giant pieces of electrical equipment, assaulting the crushed gravel with every footfall, gesturing wildly with his arms. It looked to the crew like he was arguing with someone. They could hear him shouting. Then they saw Frank kick the chain link fence that kept citizens away from the dangers of high voltage. They saw the fence absorb the energy of Frank's kick and return it to him per the laws of physical science, knocking him down to the grit of the gravel, leaving him to flail on the ground like a bad child needing discipline. They saw him lying there, eventually still. What they could not see, however, was the dark and heartless idea that had just reentered Frank's mind: something from his past, sparking anew.

"Atta boy, Franky!" he said aloud to himself while still on his back. "There you go!"

The new school year started not long after Frank's switchyard epiphany. It was sign-up time for the Cub Scouts. He decided to enroll his youngest son, and to become a den leader himself. His official story had to do with being supportive of his son's interests, and playing an active role. People bought it. Frank's garage became the home of a new den of nine Cubs, who assembled there every third Thursday to earn merit badges the Frank Pierce way. The first den meeting came off with precision, as did the second. The third meeting introduced a new theme.

"Okay," instructed Frank, "Now listen up so I don't have to repeat myself. Tonight we're gonna begin a project to show how electricity works. Doesn't that sound great?"

The boys offered no response, other than their complete attention.

"Right. So. The thing we're gonna make is called a circuit tester. Okay? A circuit tester."

Frank interprets the nine blank looks as a challenge to his authority, which makes him angry inside. And vindictive. And secretly justified in executing his true plan.

"Alright, I want you to find a work partner and pair up. And since there are nine of you, the odd man will team up with me for a special project. Now then," said Frank as he gestured toward his workbench. "Come over here to get the parts you'll need to get started. The housing is a wooden box that contains all the electrical components. Tonight I just want you to focus on gluing together your wooden boxes. We've got all the parts already cut out, and enough glue for everyone. Questions?"

After a quiet moment of shared uncertainty among the Cubs, the garage suddenly erupts into a cacophony of questions that instantly frustrate Frank. But within a few hectic minutes, the boys in blue and gold settled into their work. This allowed Frank's attention to shift back to his actual intent: to show people the importance of understanding how things work, so they could appreciate why things happen the way they do from a scientific, empirical perspective. That was his ridiculous premise for what came next.

Frank grabbed a flashlight from a ledge above his workbench, then turned to look down upon the ninth Cub Scout—the one who got stuck being Frank's partner.

"Our special project is outside, and involves the batteries in this flashlight."

Frank took the young Cub by the hand and exited the garage into the breezeway. He clicked on the flashlight, and led the boy into the blackness of the backyard, onto to the path leading to Frank's small barn out back.

Thirty-three years can go by in an instant for many people as they age. This was not true for Frank Pierce. He retired from the BPA, receiving a golden transformer statuette for his service. He never remarried. His life had become a meaningless, repetitive nothingness. The highlight for most days was getting a meatloaf sandwich for lunch at the tired-looking coffee shop he preferred. He was one of the regulars, which meant the other regulars talked about him in hushed tones.

One Tuesday, two middle-aged women sat in the booth furthest from Frank and out of earshot. One was the matronly waitress on an unauthorized break. The other was a customer of the same vintage, who always wore something pink and tipped too much.

"He's here almost every day," said the waitress. "Always in the same booth, always eating the same damn thing."

"That's what you said," said the pink lady. "But doesn't it kinda creep you out? Having him around?"

"Sure, at first. But I got used to him, and he tips almost as good as you. Besides which, I hear his whole family abandoned him, over what I don't know. So I kinda feel sorry for the old son-of-a-bitch."

"You don't know? Oh honey, I thought you knew."

"Know what?"

"He's a molester!" said the pink lady in a mock whisper.

"What, him!?"

"Yep. A Cub Scout den leader gone bad."

"No!"

"No lie. They say he got away with it for years before anybody got wise. They say the cops could never get him."

"Kids from around here?

"They'd be all grown up now, and nobody knows for sure who he messed with anyway."

"Well," said the waitress with miscalculated drama. "I guess that's an uncomfortable subject around here then."

"Sure used to be, and I really can't believe you never heard about this. Of course it's old news now. The last thing I remember hearing, it was about how his grown sons don't ever come around to see him. Not at all."

"That sounds about right, I guess," said the waitress.

"I guess."

"The bastard."

"Yeah, right."

"You know, I think the quality of service in this little diner is about to start going downhill for him."

"The bastard."

Gwen

Her four boys were due to be back in school, giving Gwen the space and time to think things through, to take stock of herself and her life, such as it was. She needed to decide what to do about how she'd been feeling since that night in late July when they all saw that miraculous green orb moving across the valley sky. She needed to pray for guidance.

She wondered how the world could go on as before. She feared with increasing ferocity that it could not, would not, and should not.

As had long been her practice on Wednesdays, Gwen packed a sack lunch for herself and Frank. She slid into her black Galaxy 500 and drove down to the substation, where Frank would normally greet her at the front entrance. This time he did not. They typically sat together in the lunchroom on rainy days and out on the front steps on nice days, sharing whatever version of soup and sandwich she'd prepared. They usually talked about the small topics of the day. And then, when the food was gone, Frank routinely walked Gwen back to her Galaxy. They systematically said good-bye with unimportant kisses.

But this time, there was no kiss. In its place was Frank's complaint about how she forgot to bring paper napkins with lunch, then her asymmetrical response.

"I'm going to do something a little different this afternoon," said Gwen.

"Atta girl!" said Frank in mock praise. "What's it gonna be? Fabric store in Stayton. The Safeway?"

"Albany."

"Albany, huh. You *are* a wild woman."

"I'm a Christian woman, Frank. Answering the call from our sister church to help finish on a quilt for someone in need."

"Uh-huh."

"Yes and then," continued Gwen, "since it's Wednesday, I'm going to stick around for their Wednesday night bible study."

"Like that's gonna be different than your regular Wednesday night bible study?"

"I put a casserole in the fridge, so all you and the boys have to do is pop it in the oven at three-fifty.

There's a fresh salad in the large Tupperware in the bottom of the fridge, too."

"Tuna and noodles with potato chips on top?"

"You'll have to add chips if you want them."

"Life is good!"

"If you say so," said Gwen with her head turned away from Frank.

"What was that?"

"It's time to go."

The steering wheel of her Galaxy had never been gripped so hard. Her whitewall tires had never forced themselves upon the hapless gravel road with such conviction. In place of a final kiss, there was only this clandestine kiss-off.

At the point where the gravel substation road met the paved highway, the Galaxy would normally turn left to go home. But Gwen steered right. After traveling a few brisk and blurry miles through farm land, she used her right hand to unfold a road map. Her eyes quickly identified the route she'd previously marked out. From the substation down Highway 226 to Scio. Then Crabtree. Then onto Highway 20, which took her directly into Albany, where she got onto Interstate 5 southbound. She drove 452 miles, stopping only for gasoline and to pee. She took the Clearlake exit and then drove 79 miles west on California's version of Highway 20. That road intersected with US 101, on which Gwen continued south until she got to Ukiah. A broad wooden sign on the outskirts of town read: Welcome to Ukiah – Home of The People's Temple.

Reverend Jim had come west from Indiana, bringing with him a message of hope for the devastatingly hopeless souls who'd struggled in vain to find their own sorry way. Gwen knew her own jarring truth all too well: that despite her saintly ways, she'd teetered on the precipice of disabling fearfulness long before ever seeing the green light in the night sky. She'd only managed to hold off the grim effects of her own spiritual gravity by distracting herself with domestic life, by doing everything there was to do with speed and intensity, by speaking continuously, so as not to allow room or time for silence, which had always been the precursor to her fears. She'd kept the totality of her personal crisis a secret from everyone.

Fear drove her to Reverend Jim. Fear inspired her to hand over the keys to her Galaxy, and to forsake all otherworldly possessions for the good of her new church. Fear helped her rationalize the decision to evaporate from the lives of Frank and the boys, and to become little more than a distinctly painful memory for each of them—she'd become a symbol of *a religion too far* for the community she left behind.

The community she had run to embraced her. It was mostly poor. It was largely black. It did not know the meaning of matriculation. So Gwen, being a reasonably educated white woman who'd experienced what most of the Ukiah faithful considered a better life, had instant standing. Credibility. Position. And, because she was still of child-bearing age, one of the positions she found herself in was on her back in Reverend Jim's bed, ready to receive his blessings, as had several women before her. The price of salvation, they each believed.

The membership of The People's Temple dined communally in a structure resembling the grange halls of Gwen's childhood. It was always crowded with people at various stages of entering, falling in line to fill their plates, eating at long tables, and then scraping off their soiled plates into garbage cans as they exited. Gwen often sat and ate alone, as was the case on the day she finally wrote a letter to her friend.

Dear Lilly,

I almost don't know how to begin this. Because even though you're a bright, young woman, I'm afraid you may struggle to understand why I did it. Especially the part about leaving Frank and the boys a few months ago. But you know me, sweetie. When all else fails I put my faith in the Lord.

The truth is, the Lord has everything to do with my decision to leave. I needed to get closer to Him however I could, because my religion was about to give out on me. Everyday Christianity was no longer enough for me. And no amount of everyday church was ever going to help me come to terms with what we all saw in the night sky last summer. Lilly, for me it was like seeing my own burning bush!

Now I know you had no sense of this, but I was in big trouble a long time before we saw the green light. For years! And seeing that thing was just too much for me. I had to find a new and better kind of religion. And that's exactly what I found here, where there's a stronger bond. And where there's a leader who didn't die for my sins. Instead our leader walks among us. Imagine! A leader we can touch, in the flesh. I'm telling you, honey, this is exactly the kind of thing I needed to restore my faith. And calm my fears.

I hope you understand.

Love,

Gwen

Gwen was with the group when it eventually moved into San Francisco, where it earned civic kudos while simultaneously refining its secret rituals. And then, years later, Gwen helped the membership organize its move to a huge leased acreage in the northern part of South America, in Guyana. That's where one of her many responsibilities was to train the reluctant in the ways of mass salvation: drinking special Kool-Aid. A photojournalist's camera exposed the abrupt finality of it all—Gwen as one among many bloated, rotting bodies in the jungle sun.

Jim

Jim looked at himself in their dismal bathroom mirror one workday morning in January, preparing to shave under inadequate light. Before the blade touched his tired face, he made the mistake of all mistakes—the kind rarely made by older, wiser people in times of trouble. His youth and dour disposition let him utter the words he would soon regret.

"Well, I don't suppose things can get any worse."

He'd spent much of the night unable to sleep, and sat instead at their kitchen table in the dark: a messy-haired statue in striped pajama bottoms, elbows on the green Formica table, chin resting heavily on the tight knot formed by his muscular hands, his straight, white teeth taking random dry bites of finger flesh and then releasing.

Lilly's day-old newspaper rested within reach on the table, folded in half and in no need of reading light— it was no friend of Jim's. His illiteracy had kept him from the facts about the green fireball as reported months before. There had been no mention of it on Cronkite, his singular source of news. There had been lunchroom chatter at the mill for a while, but Jim didn't participate. He and Lilly had touched on it a couple of times, too, though she didn't seem any more willing to delve in than Jim. Still, the thing stayed with him.

He'd seen what it had done to the Pierces and their prosperous life, and he took it as evidence that nothing good would come of what they had all seen together. He believed there was no use in trying to be hopeful for the future, because there were just too damned many things in this world that were going haywire: too many examples of defeat and despair, too many bad people doing bad things and getting away with it, too much suffering. There were too few good answers—maybe no good answers, maybe none at all.

Bleak January weather wasn't helping matters. There was neither snow, nor dramatic rain, nor tree-snapping wind, nor treacherous ice, nor—heaven forbid—clear blue skies. There was just cold fog in the morning, and low gray cloud cover all day. No matter where he was, or what he did, Jim lived under the most insidious kind of cloud, one of his own making.

Saying those bleary and unwise words into the bathroom mirror fit right into that unpromising pattern of tempting fate. Things could indeed get worse.

First, his pick-up wouldn't start that morning as he tried to leave for work. Dead battery.

"Damn it all," he said to the morning fog.

Jim had to knock on the neighbor's door to get a jump. Then, with his pickup running at last, Jim shot down the two lane highway toward the mill, anxious about not punching in late and frustrated by his own breath, which fogged the inside of the windshield and magnified the problems presented by the fog outside the pickup. He grabbed the small cloth pouch of tobacco he kept handy for such conditions and wiped a temporary circle of view on his translucent windshield, trying to conquer the reforming fog. Just then Jim entered a blind curve in the road with too much speed.

There was no opportunity to avoid hitting the yellow lab, which was spun hard by the pickup's front right bumper. By the time Jim got stopped, he could barely see the dog in his rear view mirror. He rolled down his window and crushed the transmission into reverse. With gears whining and engine roaring, and with no thought of on-coming traffic in the fog, Jim backed up to the wounded dog. The lab's hindquarters were flat on the pavement. But the confused animal was up on its front legs, looking right at Jim with eyes that simply asked why all this was happening. Its tailed wagged with false happiness. Its tongue licked Jim when he picked the animal up from the pavement and put him in the bed of the pickup. Its eyes remained hopeful each time Jim glanced over his shoulder and through the back window at the dog as he drove on toward the mill, hoping his shift foreman would okay the idea of Jim finding the dog some help.

"Maybe I can get Dutch to let me take some time to find a goddamed vet," said Jim to the two-lane highway through the windshield. "He likes dogs. Pretty sure he likes dogs."

The yellow lab died before Jim bounced into the mill parking lot. The issue with the foreman was no longer about whether Jim could take personal time. It was about the fact that Jim was already late. Recognizing the weakness of his position, Jim left the dog cold and alone.

"I'm sorry," said Jim as he walked by the bed of the pickup toward the mill. "I got no choice."

That downhearted day was measured in loads of veneer on the forks of Jim's lift truck. He spoke to no one. The few who knew him well could tell by the look in his eyes that it was best to leave Jim alone.

Let him do his job. Let him be. Catch up with him later, when conditions seem more favorable, even though there was something important to discuss in the here and now.

Jim used the isolation he'd created to roil in a sickly repetitive chain of bleak daydreams. Those paths of thought drew him in with demonic magnetism, forcing him to visit and revisit bad situations that had been real enough, and then imagined situations that deviled him just the same.

Some small part of Jim stayed on the job, allowing him to function. The bigger part punched out early, choosing instead to wander without purpose through the metaphoric forest of gloom he imagined: through the wicked and forbidding underbrush that resisted passage, with dead briars grabbing at his pant legs, with sprawling sword ferns reaching out to paint him wet with the cold rain they'd caught, with devil's walking cane doing its damnedest to prick and sting him, with viney maple throwing up roadblocks to his every move forward, with a forest floor of dank and sodden debris from things that survived for a season but then surrendered to the inevitable, with no view of the sky above because the canopy said no and meant it. It was a grim and decomposing forest of lonely despair, and Jim was its fearful detainee all day long.

The shift ended with an hour of useful daylight remaining. Weary and numb, Jim thought to salvage dignity for himself and the yellow lab by giving it a proper burial somewhere. Make amends with the beast, he reasoned. Make amends for at least this one day.

He borrowed a shovel off a log truck that sat dismantled in the nearby mechanic's shop, knowing it wouldn't be needed before morning. He fired up the pickup and headed for the filbert orchard he'd driven past every day since. He took a dirt road that disappeared into the courtly rows of leafless trees, then found a spot in the middle where a giant Douglas fir grew mighty above the nut-bearing masses. He chose a spot beneath the conifer that seemed unlikely to offer roots of resistance. Jim plunged the shovel into the dark, dense dirt and lifted slices of earth, eventually crafting a fine hole. He tucked his new dead friend down deep and comfortable, gentle and respectful, petting golden fur and asking forgiveness as dusk crept toward darkness.

Driving home, once again in the fog, Jim wept on his steering wheel. Pulling up and shutting down the motor, he stepped down from the cab and felt unsure about what came next. About putting one foot in front of the other. About getting to his own back-door. About entering the kitchen and being worthy of an evening with his Lilly, who'd demonstrated an incomprehensible ability to take his darkness without succumbing to it herself.

The small house was warm and offered the arresting sweetness of her scent. Jim sat in the wobbly wooden chair just inside the door, where there was a braided throw rug—his temporary island—to receive his boots. He sat a little longer in his stocking feet, elbows on his knees, motionless, staring at a potholder on its hook above the stove.

"Goddamned dog in the road," muttered Jim. "Goddamned green light in the sky."

Lilly watched him from the living room, looking up from the final few pages of *The Sound and the Fury,* which she'd been reading during her pregnancy. She stood quietly, glided to the doorway separating the two rooms, then continued toward Jim, directly to where he sat. He threw his arms around her waist without looking up and rested his head on her belly. She draped her arms over him, gently. Then, for a few delicate moments, they did not move.

"You okay?" Lilly asked in a soft voice.

"Not really. No."

"I know."

"I know you know."

"Yeah, I know," comforted Lilly.

"One thing, though," said Jim in a half voice.

"Yeah?"

"Don't know what I'd do without you."

"My Jimmy."

"'Cause the truth is, I'm just not…"

Lilly quickly cut him off, giving the back of his neck a finger tap.

"Uh-uh," she said. "Don't say it, and don't you even think it. Because it's not the truth, and you and I both know it."

"But I…"

Again, she cuts him short.

"Uh-uh! No sir. I'll have none of it."

Over the course of years, Jim made modest progress at not letting the world eat him alive. But he always required Lilly's help. Right up to the point when, as an old man facing death, he needed her as if for the very first time. It was their deal. Their arrangement. And it worked out nicely.

Lilly

April is the month for trilliums in Oregon's western woods. They burst up through the muck and decay of winter with a vigor that suggests there is reason to be hopeful. They throw their three slender white petals up from the forest floor in quiet celebration, completely ignoring the fact that other plants have not yet taken the bold step away from the dead season. They are pioneers of spring. They are unobtrusive ambassadors of optimism. They are messengers who can only deliver good news. Graceful, beautiful news.

Lilly loved trilliums. She knew that when they finally appeared, there would be no going back to the hunker-down days of winter.

She taught Jim about trilliums, partly as a way to help close the gap between them as she had described it to Gwen. She taught him that when April arrives, you've got to go out and search for them amongst the trees and the underbrush. You can't hang back if you expect to see them. You've got to put yourself in a position to find them. Never mind that you're a grown-up wandering through the woods in search of small white flowers. Never mind what others might think or say. Just open yourself to the possibilities of trilliums. There is a reward if you do.

Sunday afternoon in the trillium woods. Misty jacket weather. Everything was wet, but the air was as pure and vital as it could possibly be. Lilly felt enormously alive just being there. She walked slowly through the low, green ground cover, struggling only slightly with her balance, snapping twigs and branches with each step, hearing the robin's song overhead.

Jim was at her elbow, trying not to fuss over her but ready to catch Lilly should she stumble. She spotted the first trillium, but knew that it was too far down on the ground, and that she was too pregnant to retrieve it comfortably. Jim did the honors, just as he had done nine months earlier.

They had come home from the Pierce's after seeing the fantastic green light moving across the summer night sky. Sitting there in their pickup in their gravel driveway, engine and lights off, neither knew what to say or make of it. Moments passed. The only sounds came from the engine compartment, metal and fluids cooling, muffled clicks and pops. Cars on the highway made the sound of rushing air and rubber on pavement, their headlights tunneling through the darkness of a midsummer's night. Lilly reached over and took his hand.

"C'mon," she whispered.

Lilly led Jim into the rental with the brittle siding, to the center of the unlit living room, on the large, oval, braided rug. She stopped him there. She drew near, resting her head against his chest, her arms wrapped around his waist, his arms around her shoulders, his right hand cradling her head, snugging her in. Lilly began to hum something beneath her breath. Fragments of a melody. She was not retrieving it from somewhere. She was not thinking that hard. It was not a melody she knew, yet the air from her lungs moved across her vocal chords in such a way as to yield a sound, a satisfying string of notes, that suited the moment and filled the room. Lilly began to sway slightly, taking Jim with her. Their feet remained firm at the center of the oval rug in the dark. Their bodies moved together, the way cottonwood leaves respond to an easy summer breeze. Effortlessly. And somewhere deep inside Lilly, there emerged a feeling of euphoria. An overwhelming sense of well-being. And calm. And serenity. And peace. And inspiration. Everything was right. Nothing was wrong. It was as if Lilly suddenly fit in the world around her, in the life she'd been stumbling through. She sensed a new resolve, a reason for having been born, and a refreshed confidence about having chosen a life with Jim. Somehow, seeing the green orb put things right. She required no further explanation.

Still swaying, Lilly lifted her head from Jim's chest and pulled back enough to look up at her husband. Highway headlights flashed through the living room window, across the questions in his eyes. But Lilly had enough clarity for both of them, as she always would. Enough strength, too.

Lilly stepped back.

She began unbuttoning her blue summer dress. Slowly. And with splendid purpose…

Lilly felt engorged with life as Jim handed her that first trillium in the misty woods those nine months later.

"Here you go," said Jim.

"Hmmm," purred Lilly as she took it from his hand. "You know what they say about the first trillium, don't you?"

"I bet I'm supposed to know this."

"The person who finds the first one will gain unusual wisdom and unexpected wherewithal."

"Seems to me you already have more than your share of that, but okay."

They continued deeper into the woods, moving from one noble trillium to the next, Jim gathering and Lilly carrying the growing bouquet. A few moments passed in silence before Jim stopped briefly to ask his wife a familiar favor.

"'Spose maybe later, if you're not too tired, we could work on my reading a little?"

"Sure, Jimmy. Seems like a good day for it. Of course!"

"Good, because I feel like I'm starting to get the hang of it, you know?"

"I'm so proud of you."

"Yeah, right."

"Completely proud, and my only regret is that I can't brag about you to anybody, because that's what I want to do."

"But you won't."

"Only because we made a deal, you and I."

"On the other hand," said Jim. "There's a part of me that wouldn't mind having people know I finally learned how to read a little, and how to write more than my own name."

"Yeah?"

"Yeah, but that doesn't really work," reasoned Jim. "Because first they'd need to know I can't read, and there'd be a fuss about that."

"Which would embarrass you, right?"

"E-M-B-A-R-R-A-S-S."

"Look at you!" exclaimed Lilly with pride. "Do you realize there are people who've been to four-year colleges who can't spell that word?"

"Well, I *have* been taking some night classes I guess."

"The College of the Kitchen Table—I love that program."

"Yep, I crack the books where we break the bread."

Lilly stopped suddenly. She looked down to the ground, then up directly into Jim's eyes.

"You know," said Lilly in a voice that gave Jim no clue of what was happening. "I think maybe we've got something more than broken bread to think about right now."

"Say what?"

Lilly's water had given way in the misty trillium woods. And though momentarily concerned about her whereabouts, she quickly gave in to a spontaneous laughter that had a far greater need to emerge than did the baby. It was the sound of complete joy. Not so much a belly laugh, because her belly was fully occupied. But a high, trilling sort of laugh, as if made by a chorus of birds in the canopy. It filtered through the trees, and carried on the breeze. And it made the woods even more magical than they had been before. It made Lilly feel as though she'd been lifted off her feet, allowing her to all but levitate out from beneath the tapestry of treetops—she and Jim gliding away together, laughing together, out to the pickup on the road.

Jim slammed her door shut, sending tympani shockwaves back out through the trees. It began to rain as Jim accelerated on the backwoods track. Gravel flew up behind them—a few random pieces offered a sharp bang as they struck the inside of the pickup's rear wheel wells. Soon, they were on the two-lane highway, driving in full rain, windshield wipers slapping with conviction.

"You okay over there, Mister?" asked Lilly.

"Me!? You're asking about me?"

"Oh well, I really don't think I could be doing much better myself. I mean look at me: heading to the hospital to have my first baby, riding along in a great old pickup, listening to the wipers keep perfect time. Plus, I've got my guy taking really good care of me. So I just don't think I could ask for anything more. Especially since we already found..."

Lilly's first contraction came much faster than the doctor had projected, clipping her last sentence, causing her to gasp, which instantly morphed into a giggle.

"Christ Almighty!" yelled Jim in spontaneous response.

"Are you praying or cussing?"

"I'm not sure."

"Well, I suppose under the circumstances," continued Lilly. "Either is permissible."

"Thanks. But my God, that came on fast."

"Jimmy?"

He looked away from the chaotic windshield and the shiny-wet highway, directly into her eyes.

"We're gonna be fine. I know it now."

Her mate's cool-yet-attentive focus got her safely to the hospital. But it was her own true and fearless spirit that saw her through the birth of her first child.

Five days later, while nursing her baby in the room with the braided rug, that melody came back to Lilly—the one that emerged on that very same rug on that July night nine months prior. And this time it came from her memory. Now more complete. More complex. More real. She began once again to hum it.

The music stayed with Lilly throughout the rest of her life. New melodies came easily. And later, words began to emerge that made the notes make even better sense. She taught herself to score music, using number two pencils on coarse brown notebook paper. Even the sound of lead on wood pulp suggested rhythms to her. Everything was a source. Everyone had the potential to become a story in song.

Lilly gave birth to two more babies. And by the time her children were distracted by the mysteries of their own lives, she'd written more songs than could easily be recalled. She'd written happy songs for each of her offspring, of course. And thoughtful songs for Jim and his pickup. And for the dog with no name he'd had to bury. She also wrote songs for the children of Frank and Gwen, who were forced to live lives they did not want. Lilly wrote nothing for Frank, because she thought the worst of him even though she quietly held fast to the notion that there must be something good buried deep inside the man. But perhaps her best song was written for Gwen, the friend who went away and couldn't make it back home. She called it "Ukiah Wild".

Years later, with her kids grown and gone, and with her life threatening to become less than fulfilling, Lilly mustered the courage to perform her songs on the amateur talent stage in the oak grove at the Oregon State Fair. The white wooden benches were mostly empty when she began. But by the second song, people with snowcones and curly fries began stopping. By the fifth song, they were filling the benches. And then, when she performed "Ukiah Wild" as her gentle finale, Lilly's world took a crazy turn.

Overflowing curly fries fell to the ground. Snowcone remnants were tossed aside. Fleshy summer hands clapped together. Applause rose up from the white wooden benches. Whoops and whistles punctuated the oaks. She had it. And the fairgoers knew it. Felt it. Witnessed it first hand.

Lilly looked out from behind the microphone in disbelief. She looked out into the eyes of those who'd just been given a gift, and who were saying thank-you the only way they knew how. She tipped her head in awkward recognition. She banged her guitar into the microphone stand as she tried to make her exit to the familiar comfort of anonymity. But before she got ten feet from the stage, a stranger approached.

"A moment of your time, ma'am?" asked the wiry, weary-looking man in a white shirt and bolo tie.

"Hello," said Lilly.

"Ma'am, if you don't mind, I've got to tell you, I figured my best days were behind me. But after hearing those songs of yours, well ma'am, maybe I was being hasty. The name is Miles Creighton, ma'am. Nashville."

"I'm Lilly Thompson, and you're a long way from home."

"Yes, Miss Lilly Thompson, it would seem that way, wouldn't it. But when I hear music like yours, I feel at home no matter where I am."

"Thank you, Mister Creighton."

"Miles, please," he said as he adjusted his tie and moved slightly closer. "Now I don't want to hold you up any longer than it takes to ask you a simple question."

Lilly felt herself taking a tiny half-step back in response. She looked hard into his eyes, trying to anticipate a question she couldn't.

"Yes, well," said Miles Creighton, collecting himself. "Lilly, have you ever considered selling your songs? Into the music industry, I mean. That thought ever cross your mind?"

"Well I, no. I never..."

"I ask," he interrupted. "Because that's what I do. Find songs for Nashville, I mean. For the industry."

"Me? You want me to write songs for Nashville?"

"Yes, ma'am, I do. But it's not my call, you understand. I'm just the fella who opens doors. Important doors, if you know what I mean."

"Huh," said Lilly, trying to grasp.

"And I was thinking my best days were behind me," said the man with a grin.

"Yeah, me too."

The sun shone straight down on the round-topped, gray-metal mailbox that marked the juncture of the two-lane country highway with the Thompson's gravel driveway. Lilly reached to pull the drop-down door open with a leathery hand that reflected the many years that had passed since that day at the fair. She grabbed the contents, shut the mailbox door with firm resonance, and pivoted to retrace her steps out the driveway from their handsome home. But rather than entering the front door, she meandered across the vivid green lawn and around the corner of the house, thumbing through the mail.

"Anything for me today?" asked a now much older Jim, hunched over a sprinkler head in the yard, doing a repair, a rambunctious puppy at his side.

"Let's see," said Lilly as she drew nearer. "A flyer from Troybilt tractors."

"Got one."

"An oil change special from the Chevy dealer."

"Did it myself."

"Your newsletter from the goldpanners club, that's about it."

"Save that newsletter for sure," said Jim as he rebuffed the pup's attempts to help. "And what's in there for you today?"

"Oh, the regular bills and stuff. And a check from Tennessee."

"Love those checks from Tennessee!"

Lilly shifted her attention from the mail to the puppy, whose playful persistence amused them both.

"Got a name for that dog of yours yet?" she asked. "Can't keep calling her dog, you know."

"As a matter of fact I do," answered Jim as he stopped his task in favor of a better topic. "Thought I'd call her Gwenny."

"Hmmm, I like it!"

"Good ol' Gwenny."

Lilly had many more song credits by then than most people ever knew. Far fewer knew how many of her songs were written for Jim—the man whose company she always preferred, and whose weaknesses inspired some of her best work. Those songs told the story of their life together, often revealing how they overcame their obstacles, youthful and otherwise, to happiness.

Jim died when Gwenny the pup was just three. Lilly wrote him yet another song. It was about a good man who tried hard to live right and stay happy, but who was humbled by the ordeal of it all. The first lyrics for "*I'm Your Mine*" had started coming to her one day after she'd retrieved still another newsletter from the gold-panners club. She had drifted into the kitchen with it, found a pencil on the counter, and scratched out these words on the backside for the last song she ever wrote:

Don't make me be your everything,
or be the essence of your dreams.
Your turned up collar 'gainst the breeze
Your shady spot beneath the trees.

Just let me be,
what you are to me.
And soon you'll see,
together means free.

'Cause, Honey. I'm your mine.
Yes, Baby. I'm your mine.

Fifty-three years had passed since Lilly, Jim, Frank and Gwen saw the curious green light in the night sky. A hulking SUV emerged from among high mountain pines on a brown dirt road, churning up plumes of weightless and ethereal dust. It stopped beside a newer log home situated in the afternoon shadows of those lakeside trees—Lilly bought it two years after Jim passed. She appeared at the front door wearing jeans and pale blue cotton shirt. Gwenny, now full-grown and well fed, stepped into the doorway as well, eager to know who had just arrived.

"Hello! Hello, everyone," called out Lilly in what used to be her come-home-for-supper voice. "Get out of that thing and come on in. Welcome to the Ritz made of sticks."

Two of her three grown children stepped down from the SUV looking road-weary, but still happy: Jeffery, the oldest, and Catherine, the youngest.

"Well hello, Momster," said Jeffery as he swooped in to give Lilly a hug that circumnavigated her upper torso. "Good to see you!"

"Oh goodness," replied Lilly, happily overwhelmed by his zeal. "Words can't describe how wonderful it is to see you! And you, Miss Catherine! Look at you two!"

Catherine joined the scrum of affection in the thin, high mountain air, amid the trees and the swell of memories that bonded them together as a family forever in flux. Gwenny's wet nose poked in between knees to remind everyone that she, too, had a place in all of this.

"Momma," said Catherine. "I've missed you so much, and you look as awesome as ever. Who'd know you're turning seventy-three?"

"I know," said Jeffery. "I keep telling her it doesn't seem right that she's living up here, alone in the mountains, where nobody can see what a catch she'd be."

"Oh now, I think the world's seen quite enough of me," said Lilly. "And I'm far from alone, what with Gwenny here. And my music."

"Gwenny doesn't count, Mom," said Catherine. "You know what he means."

"Well don't tell Gwenny that," said Lilly. "Besides, I might not be as alone as you think up here—I've got a friend or two who come around."

They continued moving toward the door of the cabin locked arm in arm, their footsteps badly out of cadence.

"And speaking of coming around," said Lilly with a shift of tone. "It's too bad about your sister."

"We tried hard to get her to come this time, " said Catherine.

"We really did," added Jeffrey. "But you know how she can be, and it's probably for the best anyway."

"She's just so much like Daddy sometimes," said Catherine. "Makes it really tough to even have her around."

"Well," said Lilly with a well-rehearsed philosophical perspective. "Your father found his way through those dark woods, and all we can do is pray for the same for your sister, right?"

"Right," echoed Jeffrey. "Nobody can do it for her. But she did pitch in on your surprise, which I should go get out of the truck right now."

"Yes, let's not string this out," said Catherine. "Let's do this now!"

Inside the many-windowed cabin, natural light flooded the great room that Lilly had filled with the artifacts of her surprising life. The family photos, of course. And the few small things people often manage to keep from their own childhood, such as her first King James Bible, and a ceramic figurine of a kitten dressed as a pirate with an eye patch. Her guitar leaned in the corner of the room, ready. One set of three built-in shelves held Lilly's awards for writing music: That Nashville stuff, she called it.

"Here you go, Mom," said Jeffrey as he sat a large, wrapped box on the floor in front of Lilly, who had taken a seat in her leather arm chair. "Open it up!"

"Jeffrey has his knife if you want it, Mom," said Catherine. "We got a little carried away with the ribbons and Scotch tape."

He opened his pocketknife and handed it to Lilly, who then proceeded to slice where needed, quickly revealing the truth of the moment—her children had given her a telescope.

"It's a Celestron, Mom," offered Catherine. "And a good one."

"It magnifies up to 200 times," added Jeffrey. "So it oughta get you out there pretty good."

"We did a lot of research on it," continued Catherine. "And we really hope it's the right kind for what you want to do."

"You guys have really outdone yourselves," said Lilly with that voice of approval that a mother reserves for her children in their best moments. "This is perfect! Absolutely perfect!"

"We can get it all set up in time for you to use it tonight," said Jeffrey with childlike eagerness. "Tripod and all!"

"I couldn't ask for more," said Lilly. "And you know what? I just realized this isn't an it. It's a him. And I believe I'm gonna call him Leo."

Three nights after Catherine and Jeffrey had gone back to their homes and lives, Lilly had already had enough time to become familiar with Leo and his ways. She sat the impressive white telescope up on the deck outside the cabin as the stars began to appear each evening, with a stool for herself.

And there she sat. Night after night for more nights than seemed to matter, always with the warmth of Gwenny at her feet. She searched the crystalline night sky, looking for little hints of green—little glints of emerald color that held the promise of helping Lilly make sense of the life she'd been living. She looked for those little reminders of everything that was possible, for those precise little tools that helped her understand, and remember.

The people.

The events.

The way things turned out.

TEN YEARS DEAD

I WATCHED THE TALL, AMBLING man with two first names descend the forgotten, light-dappled nowhere road that parted the alders, cutting deep into the steep, shadow-green slope just above the spot where the vengeful, rock-scouring river got back to being a river, no longer a hostage to concrete and the Army Corps of Engineers. I'd been there with him before—there and everywhere else he'd been in the ten years since my death.

George Howard never wept for me, or for himself. Yet he memoried me with nearly every breath, nearly every time he went reflective, nearly to the point of perpetual numb. He pulled at me as he might drag saw teeth through the fibers of a fire log, with no intention of surrender, grip-a-grappling hard at the memory of us briefly together, then nearly together, then not together at all, except in a way he could not perceive. He was unwilling to allow himself even a flicker of life full and aglow. George was forty-seven by then, and his heart pumped an emptiness throughout, a ghost blood. I figure that affliction had swirled about since his blue-faced birth, but it got mountainous after me.

He boot-crunched out of the alders and into the rushing, roaring aura of a river that felt resentful after having been held at bay. Big Cliff Dam towered to his right as George stood agape at the dark green churn of rapids reborn. He'd followed the crushed rock of the road he'd chosen right onto the log abutment that anchored one end of a primitive bridge that was priceless during dam construction and then worthless when the reservoir went full pool. These stacks of interlocking logs sat on opposite sides of the erosive river, unsentimental giants from another time, cut down and oriented anew. Some still had their bark, their strength, and their heady, windswept memories of a life in the sky.

The logs formed a three-sided box that had been back-filled with the same sort of soil and stones that had once been home to their roots. The dirt had been tamped in with a fervent purpose, tight to the logs and the riverbank that served as the fourth wall of the box abutment. It was, altogether, a formidable construction, and it intrigued the man who was my true love, but never my lover. He claimed it as a stage for the quiet drama that hit its marks and nailed its lines in his troubled head—George trying to figure out why things went catawampus for him, why he always felt as if he'd gotten it wrong, why he felt so out of step with the dance he sometimes wished he'd never been born into.

Unanswerable questions were George's weakness. As was I.

This last time he stood there, though, his posture was different than the times before. Usually he put his hands cold-water-deep in his pockets, straight-armed and strident; his feet close together and square beneath him, his jacket pulled circus tent taut over his square shoulders by frustrated fists powering downward, his wavy haired head tilted forward, his farm boy eyes squinted at the rebirthing of rapids. Yet this time his head was up and his unpocketed hands perched on his hipbones. His eyes were not lost in the waters, but rather searched the narrow-slit sky of the deep river canyon, dancing along the gray-green silhouette of the earth's edge—trees high above on the ridge—against the pale mists that sometimes linger between western Oregon rains.

It wasn't so much that George Howard was ready for what happened next; still, it was time he came to terms with his lot. And so, with the steadying and resolute tutelage of those who wait with me just beyond perimeters of easy earthly perception, I began it.

George's first sensation was akin to the one he knew as a mile-a-minute child in his family's two-storied, lap-sided, green-shingled farmhouse when he raced down the stairs with his hand sliding on the polished clear fir banister. That's when the nerve endings in his palm bamboozled his brain into thinking that perhaps he was falling, because he lacked grip, and it gave him that floating, fluttering, flying feeling on the soft flesh between his elbows and his armpits, and again inside his birdcage ribs. His instincts did not care whether it was fun or danger or that liquorous place in between. All he got was the nettled rush of sudden descent.

I watched him fall as the abutment caved in.

Down where the dirt used to be, down inside the log box, suddenly a hungry hole swallowed George whole with no more sound than that of a down comforter being fluffed over a sensual woman's bed, and with no more effort than a hibernating bear grunt-shifting slightly in its seasonal sleep. The hole had him. It was quick, deep and dark.

The box had a partial bottom, and that's where George landed on his back, on top of ancient rocks of the riverbank. They were round and raspy to the touch, long shrouded in the blackness of the dam builders' handiwork. He saw nothing at first, and did not move; he could not breathe. The air that had been squeeze-tubed from his lungs was petulant about returning. When it finally did, only then could George begin the unpuzzling.

Above him, a bright orifice loomed. Maybe twelve, maybe fifteen feet above where he lay supine and undone.

Beneath him, between his spidered-out legs, there was another opening. Smaller. Darker. Much less welcoming. And through that menacing hole—still large enough for a man's body to fall through—he saw the livid river. More than that, he felt it. It smelled simultaneously fresh and putrid. He feared it.

George moved not a twitch. Rather, his brain flailed to deconstruct the sequence the floodwaters had begun those ten years before. Calm came in the figuring out: how the crazed currents of time and high water undercut the bank that held the abutment, how the triumvirate of hydraulics and erosion and persistence assaulted the backfill, how the solid mass of dirt and rock inside the log box morphed into a cavernous trap, how the dirt on the surface was the last to go, how his one-hundred-ninety-three pounds were the difference, how he fell into dank and solitary confinement, and how he wasn't likely to escape. This last realization undid all the calming.

George head-scratched whether moving would make things worse, considering how unstable the remaining dirt might be. He stared down the river sphincter. He looked at the luminous torment overhead, blinding himself to all but this urgency:

How the hell am I gonna get outta here?

I happied at that particular question. It meant he wanted survival, and I'd always questioned how much George Howard really wanted to walk this earth at all.

Blunt truth be spoken, escaping that cave-in was pissdribble compared to the whirlpool uncertainty of escaping the hole he'd shoveled for his own soul.

That's why I steered him here to this spot time and again. Why the river did my bidding, and why the earth gave way to the excessive weight of his woe. It was all to help him jettison the ballast of a life poorly lived, so that he might come to know buoyancy.

George.
Hello, George.

He heard me speak to him, but did not respond.

> *It's me, George.*
> *Jane.*
> *I'm here with you.*
> *George?*

His eyes battled darkness to see what his ears saw: the voice of the only woman he ever truly loved, coming to him amid the cloistered roil of the river, surrounding him from all directions.

His heart pounded like noisy upstairs neighbors, heavy-footed and indiscreet. It bass-drummed hard, echoing out of his open mouth, clicking a guttural cadence on the soft tissues of his throat.

> *It's okay, George.*
> *It's okay.*
> *You'll be fine, sweetheart.*

Still he did not answer me. He could not answer me. At least not with mouth words. But those eyes of his talked the obvious:

> *Am I going crazy?*
> *Am I dead?*

Then I said softly:

No, George.

You're very much alive.

But you need a little help just now.

I'm here to help, sweetheart.

And all you have to do for me is remember to breathe.

His lungs took in stabs of cool air on my advice. He shifted on the rocks and dirt, crabbing backward. He looked up at the hole that took him, and then glanced down at the vindictive waters. I felt his fear.

It's time, George. It's time to rest, and to remember better times.

Remember that day in the snow together?

That walk we took back along the lane, making footsteps where nobody else had been? The clean, crunching sound of our boots against the hush of falling snow?

The pink flush of our cheeks in the chill January air?

You remember. Don't you, Dear. You do.

Yes. You do.

George let himself relax, flexing his elbows to lower his back onto the ground again.

There we go. That's better.

He mattressed into the dirt and rocks. His head nested between the roundness of three rocks, cradling him as I would. The bones of his spine found a way to lie as well, each vertebrae picking its spot and judging it acceptable for the moment. His knees were bent. His feet found places to be that held him steady without requiring his attention. A calm grew from within as the constancy of moving water blended with my voice. He grew content to remember.

We fell in love that day in the snow, George.
Kinetically.
Exponentially.
Fearlessly in love.

I knew that my unabridged vocabulary wouldn't be too much for my illiterate man, and that my dime store words wouldn't frustrate him. I remembered how much he liked hearing them before, when we were younger and together. Besides, I'd become much more myself since dying. Much more literary and lyrical. And I knew, too, that the tone of my voice would get it right for him. And that his heart would interpret for his brain.

> *Sweetheart, this is going to seem harsh, but you have a choice to make now.*
>
> *It's a very big choice, and it's completely up to you.*

He remained motionless on his back. He tried to avoid looking up at the hole he'd fallen through, because the brightness hurt his pale blue eyes. He tried to avoid looking down through the hole that led to the river, because the rush and flow intimidated him. Eventually he settled into staring at the darkness, a wide-eyed child again.

> *You're thinking there's no way out.*
>
> *You're thinking you're going crazy, hearing me this way.*
>
> *But you're not crazy, George. And you're not without options. I swear.*
>
> *Just listen to me, won't you? Listen and then decide…*

George exhaled a large breath he'd been holding without intent.

Okay, here it is, my love.

If you still want the life you have, if you're willing to stick with it.

Well, there's a way out of here.

You can climb up these black walls.

There are roots you cannot see.

They're old roots, coming from a buried stump that nobody remembers.

They're strong, George, more than strong enough to bear your weight.

They're hanging down above you right now, just to your right.

You have but to stand up and reach for the roots.

You might have to jump a little.

Take them with both hands and use the strength of your arms to pull yourself up. As you do, swing your feet up. They'll find a place to land up high.

You'll gain leverage, but you'll have to fight for it.

So if you're not determined, well, this route will test you.

George, that root runs by the edge of the hole.

You can muscle your way to the opening.

The hole will open no further, so you can trust it to hold while you emerge.

You can trust me.

He strained to see the roots I described, not yet trusting.

But George, honey. There's another way out to consider.

One that'll bring you to me.

George shifted onto his side, engaged by the voice of his true love.

You can go into the river, George. You can lower yourself down to the waters.

Say good-bye to the world that has tormented you so.

Surrender to the icy depths and be carried away from all of this.

From everything. From everyone, except for me.

Because I'll be waiting for you on the other side, Sweetheart.

We'll be together forever, the way we were supposed to be.

But in a way that's far better than you ever imagined.

I can't say more than that, George. I'm not allowed.

George seemed to take in my words.

> *I'm going to leave you now, George. I'm going away so you can decide.*
>
> *It's just a decision, my love. And it's impossible for you to decide incorrectly.*
>
> *Good-bye for now.*

I lingered a moment to study the man with two first names as he pondered in the dark. One last look. And then I was away, damned aware that as George Howard decided his own fate, he'd hold sway with mine.

The Enemy of Swagger

There wasn't much to recommend the espresso stand. It was the kind of place he was prone to try when it was inconvenient to wait at a better-known place. A potential default spot, he hoped, where perhaps the lines were shorter, and the interior design had maybe never been anywhere near an architect's to-do list. Still, the coffee aroma was tolerable.

He searched the unfamiliar menu board for his drug of choice and waited to be acknowledged. Soon, there was brief eye contact, and the shy young redhead at the cash register mumbled something he took to be an invitation to order.

"Double twelve ounce Americano. Extra room. Shots on top." Those were the practiced words that under normal circumstances would get him his minimum daily requirement.

"You sure you want a double?"

The question came out of nowhere. From someone other than the pale girl taking orders and money. Distracted by the oddly folded ones in his wallet and somewhat disoriented by the new coffee setting, he was unsure where to aim his reply.

He looked up and into the neutral gaze of the patient but indifferent redhead, quickly confirming that she had not asked the question.

"Our twelve ouncer is automatically a double," said the voice. "If you get a double it's actually four shots. Just a heads-up."

"Two shots is plenty," he said in the general direction of the voice. It seemed to be coming from behind the espresso machine, which was crowned by towering stacks of upside-down paper cups of various sizes, stacked to varying heights.

Not just any voice can carry over the hiss and screech of an espresso machine—today's equivalent to the steam locomotive. Can't be a high voice. Or a weak one. It must be a formidable voice. Like a conductor hanging outside a train as it begins to move. This voice was all that, yet there was nothing about it that might cause a person to recoil. Nothing intense. Nothing piercing, just strong. Confident. Intriguing.

Like Marlene Dietrich without the accent. It was one of those voices that suggested you already knew one another. That, in fact, you knew each other quite well. You liked each other. There was a natural rhythm between you.

But he knew nothing of the woman behind the wall of cups, and something told him this situation was unlikely to change. Women like this, with voices like that, do not fit comfortably into his waking hours.

Still, he was drawn in.

It was a complex voice; it conveyed contradictory feelings. There was a quality to it that was friendly and inviting, even comforting. Yet there was another quality that acted as a kind of buffer or perimeter.

"You new?" said the voice. "I've never seen you here before."

His answer was completely unimportant. He definitely said something in response, but the details and meaning evaporated the moment they left his mouth. Her voice had taken hold.

It wasn't a deep voice, though there was a subtle resonance. It had a certain kind of low-end that probably isn't detectable to many people. Still the majority of human males, especially those who have put distance between themselves and adolescence, find voices like these more than noticeable, and sometimes even irresistible.

Enticing women undo most men. Beneath all the posturing and cool, men are still just uncertain little boys. When in close proximity to such a woman, that uncertainty wells up to the surface, quickly becoming the enemy of swagger. It acts like a virus on previously healthy tissue, nibbling at the cells of the ego, licking away wisdom and common sense, generally becoming a threat to a guy's ability to think straight.

It gets worse. Hands suddenly have no idea where to be. Clothes seem not to fit. Voices falter, often coming out higher and thinner than desired. And forget about being clever, because cleverness has left the building, destined to return only during the endless mental replays of encounters like this. In its place? Stupidity.

There is always a clock running on encounters like this. When time is up, you leave. That's what he did, trying not to be burned through the paper cup by the hot coffee, or to be revealed as a buffoon to the voice behind the espresso machine. His coffee eventually cooled, but his intrigue in the voice gained steam.

He returned to that coffee stand, day after day. He became a regular, and was taken into the fold. And best of all, he found a way to maintain his cool.

He had help, lots of it. After all, he was just one of many men who lined up at that location every morning for a cup of acknowledgement from the young woman with the voice. There were young men, middle-aged men, fathers, grandfathers, happily married men, unattractive men, athletic men, bureaucratic men, aspiring businessmen, slovenly men, quiet men, scholarly men, policemen, flirtatious men, and a few other types as well.

Each man suffered the same remarkable fate at that unremarkable coffee stand. Regardless of his station in life, each man sought a little something extra with his coffee each morning: a measure of acceptance by the woman with the voice. And she served it up—to varying degrees—in a way that made each man feel just a little bit better.

Miss Kitty with coffee, that's who she was. A woman who could intone that you were welcome, and that she was glad you stopped by. A hostess with an air of confidence and the gracious ability to do three things at once without seeming harried. A conversationalist for all who dared to match their voice against the public hissing of the steam wand, with a diplomat's ability to endure the most inane comments without so much as a roll of her eyes.

The men at the counter savored her endorsement, which might be nothing more than for her to say their names out loud for all to hear. They embraced the moment while understanding there was no way they would ever be in a position to embrace her. Even the slickest, smoothest suits were kept at arm's length by the counter and the cups and the steam and the hiss of the coffee locomotive. Even if all men were not created equal, it's certain that all men who approached this particular espresso stand were rendered equal.

Viewed from the back of the line, they often looked ridiculous, these men seeking coffee and encouragement. They were even a little pitiful. Listening to the banter, it was easy to tell when someone was new to the routine. The new ones talked too much and said too much. They asked too much and grinned too much. They reacted too much and postured too much. All of which, in turn, could be too much for the woman with the voice. So when someone crossed the line of subtlety, she deftly shifted her attention to a more deserving recipient. She did this easily, almost imperceptibly. The poor sap who'd been publicly brushed off had no idea what happened. The more astute observers of this morning melodrama knew all too well, having learned what constituted too much. This daily dialogue was like making espresso: approach it too quickly, and the result was weak and unsatisfying. Draw the approach out too long and you get bitter disappointment. Subtlety and timing prevailed.

There was a cycle here, a pattern that repeated itself daily, a light addiction. Though fulfilling and quietly satisfying at the moment of consumption, and perhaps for a few hours afterward, the need eventually announced its return. It was neither painful nor a deep longing nor an impulse. It was simply one aspect in a chain of events that had a measure of value, if not real meaning. It was something that of course could be done without. Nonetheless most of the men lined up at the counter would have struggled to come up with a good reason to go without tasting the coffee—and hearing the voice.

She was a mirage. She appeared amidst a landscape of sameness as a shimmering object. A goal. She had become a reason to put one foot in front of the other. She served incremental hope. And no matter how badly the men at the counter wanted to draw near her, she hovered beyond the limits of their reality. She was unreachable and then, suddenly, she was gone.

The espresso stand lasted another six months after the woman with the voice had moved to another city. The men at the counter went their various ways, but each of them was bound to the other by the memory of her voice.

He shared that memory with them.

But unlike the others he had something more to go on; every time he reached over the counter to take his drink from her hands, he'd managed to let his fingers touch hers. That sensation was so powerful, it all but muted her voice.

Things I Wish I Didn't Know

The metal screen door banged shut behind him as he crossed the concrete porch he'd poured back when his adopted son was little. He stepped into a daybreak rain, bound for the barn, thermos in hand. Liz had wanted a wooden porch with a railing, maybe a wooden screen door with fancy carved parts. He'd thought about it, too. But life on earth, Clay resolved without cynicism, was just a string of adjusted dreams.

With the brim of his soiled chore hat down low and the collar of his thick but threadbare jacket turned up high, he walked in a way that reflected an easy relationship with raindrops. Clay welcomed them like old friends with flaws.

Now fifty-seven, but not yet weathered, Clay was strong of grip and spirit. His poker-faced approach to everything and everyone had begun in his strapping-young days as a cover for shyness, but then evolved over the decades into blue-eyed authenticity. Liz knew his secret and loved him for it. The farm animals knew it, too. Bucket, the Border Collie at his feet, sniffing his boots in stride. Cows waiting for hay and molasses. Barn swallows rustling in the rafters and sending feathers. Rats stealing grain.

Clay was no easy read outside the barn's knot-holed walls and rusting metal roof. Inside the barn, it was another story.

Sounds of the walk from the house to the barn: rubber boots scruffing on cement, then washing through uncut grass, then crunching on gravel that shifted underfoot, then sucking through barnyard muck, then a different sort of scuffing on long-dry dirt beneath loose hay inside the barn. And then, rain drumming its fingers on the corrugated metal above.

That rain-sound resonated with his heavy mood. So much so that Clay broke the ritual of his Saturday mornings, and chose to sit down on the closed feed-box rather than doling out its contents. He poured black coffee from the thermos into the green cup that rarely departed the barn—it steamed against the chill. Then he lit a Winston, admitting to the red glow and snuffed match that he'd probably never quit even though he kept promising Liz otherwise.

"Yeah, Buckethead," he said to his dog. "Young Greg's on his way today. Gonna be interesting. Pro'bly gonna be hard."

He replayed the conversation with Liz. The one from a month before, when she announced her plan. She said it was for Greg. "He deserves to know his real father because every child does, even the grown-up ones." But Clay sensed something else, and that's what had him riled and raw.

"Greg gets in for the noon meal," she said. "Then at three or so, the other guest is due. Doesn't matter if you're for it or against it, because it's happening either way. You can be there or not. Doesn't matter. But don't be there," she warned, "if you can't get things squared away in your head. Don't be there if you can't behave."

Clay growled in the back of his throat, recalling her resolve.

Scents in the barn: the ancient dust of neglected places, rain sweet and close, acrid feces of various vintages and species, wet dog, feed grain with a richness that tickles the instinct to chew, mild mildew from everywhere, the roasty promise of coffee not long from the pot, intoxicating cigarette smoke not long from the glow, and the much-younger Liz on his fingers—one of the many reasons Clay had to give it a go with the unwanted company.

All she ever had to do was mention the man's name. That's all it took. Never mattered where they were or what they were doing. Never mattered how good a mood Clay was in, or how entranced he was by his wife of twenty-three years: the former Elizabeth Jenkins, the small-time ice skating star who nearly went Olympic.

When he heard that name, when Liz said that name in conversation, it never mattered how innocent it all was, or how meaningless. Clay tightened inside. It stopped him cold, every time.

A tiny ice dagger well thrown from the unchangeable past.

Damn sure to stick and trickle invisible blood.

Another punctured lung.

Inhaled pain.

"I just don't know what to make of those fancy pants boy skaters, Bucket," said Clay through a cumulous puff. "Don't relate to the whole idea of it. Never did. Never will."

Bucket looked into Clay's eyes with full canine compassion.

"Now girls on ice, that's something else. That's where it's at."

Bucket tapped Clay's knee with a paw, agreeing. Clay scratched Bucket behind the ears.

"Seems like you're the only one..."

His mind had drifted off like smoke, finally alighting on that big fight from years ago. The bad one. The one he should have known to avoid. But no, Clay had tried to make his case about how hard it was to be a proud man when your wife mentions men from her past, as if it was a topic he should be happy to embrace. As if he should be as comfortable as she, and just as inclined to relive anecdotal moments that he'd rather she left unshared. He'd never seen Liz so angry, so ready to end it on the strength of her righteous point of view. He remembered how she mocked and eye-rolled his point of view. Disemboweled it with her table-turning logic. And that's when Clay realized the full moon truth about the two of them as a couple: that she was stronger inside than he was.

Clay's cigarette grew short and spent. What remained of his coffee no longer steamed. His eyes locked on a knothole in the opposite wall, transfixed.

Bucket waited.

The rain picked up just then, and the change brought Clay to his feet, lifting him out of his mental eddy, bringing him to the boundary between wet and dry at the broad opening of the barn which—like the man sanctuaried inside—usually kept its back to the weather. Clay stooped to pick up a chewed stick left behind by Bucket, who had enough small nervous habits to make up for his master's lack of them. A sudden sliver was Clay's reward for such an unimportant task; it was lodged in the soft, uncalloused side of his ring finger, near the band he wore for Liz. He took out his pocketknife, opened a slender, pointed blade, and began working the irritant. It occurred to Clay that life has all kinds of slivers, that the invisible ones hurt worse, and that it would be grand if all a person ever needed to fix problems was a sharp knife and the will to use it.

"You and your damn sticks," he said to Bucket, who upon hearing one of his favorite words, ran off to find another.

By the time Bucket returned, Clay had moved back inside, where he refilled his green cup, lit another Winston, then took a seat on a bale of hay, his back against the stack of many more bales—his easy chair. The rain came down even harder.

Tastes in Clay's mouth: black coffee that lacked the encouraging qualities of the first cup, tangy smoke that now danced dangerously close to unpleasant, acidic sourness that permeated his saliva—not uncommon when he was battling ghosts from the past.

One of the heifers waiting for hay kicked the barn hard, engulfing Clay in a cavernous shockwave. He looked over his shoulder to see who was being impatient, between the slats of the v-shaped bunker that cradled the hay within reach of slobbering lips and tongues. He made eye contact with the white-face heifer. Clay exhausted more cigarette smoke. The cow exhaled a huge, whooshing breath through its nose, creating a cloud of steam that lingered long enough to send Clay thinking again.

That steam reminded Clay of translucent fabric. Of fine, delicate, gossamer trails that flowed from Liz's arms and back when she was much younger, when she was a skater on the edge of greatness. She had glided in the spotlight of aspiration; the alluring yet naive woman-child from Oregon who feared neither the weight of celebrity nor the wanton entanglements of those who watched her, wanting her.

Clay overheard Liz telling a friend about that night, believing with full conviction that her life's secrets should not be secrets at all. Not comprehending that her candor came with consequences.

That night. That man.

He'd been there competing as well. An ice dancer. Older than she. His partner's claim on him did not extend beyond the ice. There was a party after the competition. Liz wore her costume without the skates, not wanting the feeling of success to end. It was white and sheer. It sparkled and clung. It made every movement—Clay imagined—a thing of painful beauty, simultaneously innocent and arousing, teasing and crushing the heart of any man who passed within the silken weightlessness of angel wings held aloft, scenting the air and altering the space around her, casting a good spell.

Liz never referred to that night or that man as a mistake, leaving with him as she had. She had laid down in his hotel room, her snowy veils arraying around her and framing her on the bed, letting him.

Though many years removed, Clay still felt wronged—that it was that man and not himself. He knew the man was unworthy of trespassing Clay's idea of perfection. He had tread on Clay's favorite fantasy and utter fascination with the woman he loved, on Clay's sense of timelessness for Liz—his possessiveness of her in the past, the present, the future.

Clay was practical, though. He knew when he asked Liz to marry him that Greg had to come from somewhere. He knew there was a story behind it. He knew, too, that taking on the raising of the child meant bearing the burden and acceptance of the truth. This he had done, and done well for all these years. He'd put it where it had to be and got on with his business, never fully accounting for the fact that one day he'd have to meet Greg's real father. He'd never anticipated the bellychurn that this rainy day brought, this torrent inside.

Tactile sensations dominating Clay: stinging in the corners of his mouth, tightness in the upper throat, tension across his shoulders and running up the back of his neck to his skull, rawness in his unfed belly, Bucket licking his right hand, a twitching muscle in his right thigh, toes gone numb with a chill of his own making.

"Well, you planning on staying out here all morning?"

Clay hadn't heard Liz coming, so her voice made him start. She stood just outside the wide mouth of the barn, in the rain, arms crossed, her own mouth drawn tight and small by the tension of the day ahead and the question just asked. Clay did not answer. He looked directly into her eyes to take a measure of the moment and his wife, but then looked past her, into the grayness.

"Really?" pressed Liz. "You're really just gonna hide out here in the barn? Moping with your cows?"

He let the insult ricochet off his jacket and up toward the swallows, which rustled in response.

"I'm working on it," said Clay with a tone that offered a warning while also doing a pitiful job of masking his frame of mind.

Liz got wetter by the second. She finally stepped in. Clay understood that she would rather have stayed outside, and that she resented having to move in his direction. She kept her distance, and wiped a drip from the end of her perfect nose. They locked eyes again. Bucket trotted over and wagged a hello to Liz. Clay's eyes followed the dog and then noticed that she'd worn, and ruined, her slippers. She saw him looking.

"Time for new slippers, I guess," said Liz.

"Well," said Clay, not quite sure if there was room for humor. "Least you aren't wearing your skates today."

She absorbed the comment without reaction for a few seconds. Then, a voluminous sigh. She shifted her weight to one leg and let the other leg extend unbent to the side, to a point—natural choreography. She uncrossed her angular arms and then recrossed them with less force. Her brown eyes opened more fully. She sniffed.

"You know what?" asked Clay.

"What."

"I've got a pretty long list of things I wish I didn't know in this life. And it's getting longer all the time."

"Yeah?"

"Yeah. Too damn long for my tastes, let me tell ya."

"Uh-huh."

"Yeah, too damn long," Clay continued, buying time.

"Is there something you need to tell me?"

He took a moment to tidy up the thought in his mind.

"The boy deserves to know his father. I can see the wisdom of that. And maybe today's as good a day as any for that."

"But?"

"But...I just...you know..."

"If I knew, Sweetheart, it's not too likely I'd be out here right now with cow shit on my slippers. Don't you 'spose?"

Clay breathed in hard through his nose, inflating his lungs with fresh conviction.

"Liz?" he said as if asking for help. "Honey? I just can't get it out of my brain—that image—the way you described it. Damn thing keeps playing over and over—like a movie that never ends, only I didn't want to see it in the first place."

"What the hell are you talking about, Clay?"

Another silent moment.

"You mean you really don't know? You really don't have a clue?"

She shrugged her shoulders. Seeing this, Clay raised his eyebrows and rocked slightly backward for dramatic affect.

"Shit the bed, Fred! How can you not know?"

Again with the shoulders, but now her eyebrows raised as well, as a way to press him.

"Well I'll be damned..." he said, looking down at Bucket, feeling instantly unable to say it all, disheartened that Liz hadn't a clue.

The white-faced cow kicked the barn again, echoing in a way that obliterated the moment and provided the couple with their respective escape routes from the truth. Every living creature in the barn sensed it, and waited—each and every one, breathing in the missed opportunity, breathing out the barn's subtle brand of sad, graceful vapors that twirled and posed, then vanished.

Liz chose to go as well, spinning in her slippers, marching away into the rain, flipping him the finger over her shoulder at the last second.

"Asshole!" she shouted to the rainy barnyard.

Clay stayed put.

The whiteface kicked the barn a third time, prompting Bucket to get up from where he'd been laying in the hay, to check on Clay. A cold, wet nose pushed beneath Clay's arm, nudging.

"Son of a bitch," said Clay with resignation. "Damn it all to hell."

Bucket whined a reply.

"Now I gotta go in there and fix it."

Swallow your pride, said Bucket's eyes.

Clay looked down at nothing in particular on the floor, amused by the wisdom of a dog, suddenly understanding what Bucket understood, that some things ought not be over-thought.

He stood. He straightened his back and put his hands on his hips. He stretched his neck backwards to release the tension that burrowed into his muscles and tendons and vertebrae, then looked up at the rafters and mud nests of the swallows, and then back down at the hay-strewn floor. At Bucket.

"Okay. Here goes."

Clay walked to the boundary between wet dirt and dry. He stopped to feel in his jacket pocket for the Winstons, but then realized that to smoke was to stall. He let out a huge breath of steam that glided out in front of him as if to show the way.

"Hell, Bucket," he said as the two of them stepped into the rain. "Sure thought I'd be wiser by now."

Bitter Parents of Untalented Children

"Oh look," said Carol to Bill as they strolled into the hotel ballroom holding hands. "They tried for opulence again. Isn't that precious?"

"Well, I'm sure they did the best they could considering this is Oregon," said Bill. "But honestly, Darling, these decorations bring to mind the slutty, red stains of a careless cabernet."

'Yes," said Carol. "Slutty is the word for it alright."

Their seats were assigned to them by strangers who wore fashionista activewear for the event set-up and then switched to shimmering backless gowns for the event: Portland's annual Iconic Wines Auction, a cattle call of the accomplished.

Their place at the table of life, Bill and Carol realized, was often less about their own choices and more about the energies, equations and machinations of others, whose mission it was to exercise eminent domain and other social trespasses upon those with kinder spirits. Bill and Carol understood and accepted this while no longer feeling victimized. This and so much more, but only after decades of trying to live it down. Only after realizing, well past the time that their wild hair in private places had turned a disappointing shade of gray, that the *why* was inconsequential, and that *how* they chose to respond was all that mattered. They learned this together, and well, and then resolved in tandem to plot their own happy ending.

Their table at the back of the cavernous ballroom was round, surrounded by ten chairs and place settings, and unceremoniously crowded with clusters of long-stemmed wineglasses. Two other couples already took up positions facing the front of the room. Two acceptable seats remained for Bill and Carol.

All six of them were wise enough to know that it's one thing to be relegated to the back of a room containing thousands of people. It's quite another thing—a much, much worse thing—to be seated at that same table with your back to the front of the room, doomed to scrutinize white-jacketed servers bringing food, and jewel-encrusted beauties escaping beneath green EXIT signs to relieve their fragile bladders.

"You know, Dear," whispered Carol into Bill's ear. "We look like we belong at the front of the house. We look very good."

"Indeed we do, but I'm quite content in the back."

He, a trim Brit barely tall enough to reach the top shelf at the grocery store, wore gold wire-rims that sat comfortably on his slender, angular nose; a complement to the aging but professorial face of a man whose closely cropped beard and head of hair glowed white. Smile lines radiated out from his bright blue eyes. Bill was handsome in a self-contained way, owing partly to his black tuxedo, and partly—he knew—to the woman who'd been by his side for thirteen years.

Carol was three inches shorter than Bill, with the frame of a watchable bird; she was a slender redhead with delicate skin so pale and sheer, she made the whole concept of tanning seem laughable. There she was in her jewel-toned silk blouse and flattering floor-length black skirt. Carol was at that crossroad in the lives of all women, when the easy charms and cheery buoyancy of youth had not yet fully given way to the inelastic cruelties of aging. True, the dewy softness of passing decades had settled in on her complexion, signaling to those who notice these things that Carol was past the age of birthing. But she never had children. She never wanted them. She embraced and celebrated her role as baroness of barrenness. Just as she embraced and celebrated the striking man who, like her, regretfully claimed a childhood that made the idea of bringing children into the world utterly unacceptable.

The first toast they had ever shared, an Oregon pinot noir at a sunny hilltop tasting one September, was a tart and succinct acknowledgement of their mutual disdain for people who should never become parents. All children deserve better, they agreed. This is what first bound them together, this acrid truth. But then, over time and many more toasts to topics far less grim, love grew between them. Love that veiled their stricken histories in gossamer bandage of hope and forgiveness. Love that caught them and rolled them toward one another, just as gravity takes human bodies to the center of a garden hammock, prevailing and then grinning about it.

They touched each other often at the table, discreetly. Sometimes they looked into each other's eyes, other times not.

There was a rhythm between them that required neither intent nor attention. Theirs was a syncopated energy. One that diagramed around them like a magnetic field, arching gracefully from one soulful pole to the other, then radiated outward to those nearby, setting up subtle vibrations that could be detected easily by those who live life uncorked and open. Bill and Carol noticed and celebrated such openness in others at every opportunity, but harbored no judgment on those who lacked it, including the two other couples at the table.

Bill and Carol's auction paddle waited: white, round, and dominated by the number 531 in large, black type with graceful serifs — at rest between their place settings.

The rotund auctioneer on the stage up front wore a white, long-sleeved shirt beneath a multi-red satin vest every bit as loud and violent as his voice. His job was to shout at affluent people with numbered paddles, to bid up their egos, and to toy with their prestige in the name of charity.

The moneyed ones, they sat nearest the auctioneer in predetermined proximity. Their tables were neither larger nor rounder. Their glass stemware glistened no more brightly. Their white paddles were identical to the one Bill and Carol had, save for the black numerals. But the ones with money had done well in life, had made their parents proud. The price of that pride manifested in giving away tidbits of their success by flashing their paddles toward the man in the vest.

As the auctioneer bellowed over the public address system in piercing, almost machine-gun staccato, tuxedoed elves scampered between the tables to find and feature those whose paddles quivered in anticipation, holding red-coned flashlights in the air above the bidders, wiggling and waggling so the auctioneer could pick them out and then shout out a new, higher price for the lot at hand. Nobody scampered near Bill and Carol. No elves would be necessary when Bill stood to bid. He would be seen. The number 531 would be noted.

Carol doodled on the page of the program that described their lot, biding her time. The threadwork of veins on the back of her hand moved like unearthed worms as she penned out her silent ideas, content to pay only passing attention to the breathless battle of the money paddles, all but ignoring the vested bullhorn who ping-ponged from bidder to bidder. They had discussed their plan in detail, Bill and Carol. She trusted Bill to act. She anticipated their shared pride when he would stand and remain standing until he'd won, thwarting the attempts of all unsuspecting contenders, the unimpressed gentry who might not even turn their heads to the back of the room to see who'd bested them. But best them he would.

Carol sketched a desk. An old, cluttered desk with a single task light perched dead center. She drew the chair, too. Then two wineglasses. Then the bottle. The corners of her mouth lifted almost imperceptibly as she contemplated what was to come. How they would celebrate yet another triumph. How they would further heal the wounds made by the hollow expectations and miscalculations of the previous generation.

She thought of her mother as she sketched. She thought of the too many times she called Carol retarded in front of others, because the daughter had done or said something odd or awkward that embarrassed the mother. Carol remembered the many times her mother told her she was an accident, that she should have never been born, and life was burdensome enough before Carol came along to complicate things. She winced at the pinprick memory of sloughing blood trickling down her skinny leg at school, having never been told what to expect when she began the transition to womanhood, having never even heard the word menstruation.

It all swirled for Carol as she doodled in the ballroom. The crushing comments. The subtle condemnations. The endless criticisms. The brutal lies and errors of parental omission. And then there was the situation with Ray…

He was her oldest sister's husband: a selfish, boorish man in his twenties when Carol was all of eight.

Thick fingered and greasy haired, Ray smirked sideways at the world and took from it as he pleased. She remembered his odor, which triggered a wicked, coiled bedspring of nausea spiraling into her belly, digging deep with a tiny jag of ripped metal leading the way, burrowing in and then unleashing the nightmarish facts: that when Carol finally found the courage to go to her mother about what Ray was doing, there was no angry lioness in Carol's defense. She was told to keep quiet, so as not cause problems in the family. She was instructed to pretend it never happened. The woman who gave Carol life, and who should have been willing to protect her to the death, instead did nothing.

The facts piled up like empty bottles in a back alley. Carol had been aware of them for decades, and remained unable to ignore their sour smell well into her middle years. But then it came to her that even life's most retched excrement eventually dries up and loses its ability to torment the nose and dislodge the memories. And so, Carol worshipped the silence of the sweeping second hand. The sleepy gongs of the hourly chime. The rectangular days on the calendar. The years strung together like sugary beads on a candy necklace, one jostling against the next, leading her away from the numbing horrors of an imperfect childhood. Leading Carol at long last to life with Bill, who had likewise suffered in youth.

The closets in the apartment they shared had no doors. It was Bill's wish. They had removed each one, backing out Philips head screws by hand, extracting flat brass hinges and strike plates from their woody insets and setting them aside in case some future occupants might want them. Bill was calmer with the brass removed and the closet doors banished to storage.

He, too, had been banished. His scowling, vinegar-faced mother said it was all she knew to do when Bill disappointed her by failing a chore or speaking out of turn. She, who wore only shades of gray each day of her sodden life, she had been the one to teach Bill the hard, black consequences of crossing her or violating her house rules. She always framed the decision so as to portray herself as having no choice in the matter. That closet of hers it was her only option. And those words of hers: "I've taught you everything I know, lad, and still you know nothing. To help you remember, in you go."

Bill feared little in life, save for the inky isolation of being locked on the wrong side of a closet door for lifetimes at a time.

Yet in the sliver of time it took to flash back on those bleak punishments at the hands of a mother who herself lived in perpetual darkness, Bill could, with a cleansing blink of his bright blue eyes, conjure up the more sustaining truth: that for every dark closet, there is a ribbon of brilliant light fingering in between the bottom of the door and the dusty floor. This light taught Bill better lessons than his mother's sediment-laden heart ever could. It taught him to have hope. It taught him to hold out for the good things that must surely await. It also taught him to value what little good he already had, to applaud it silently but sincerely. Mostly, the slice of light taught him that good lived deep inside him, sheltered from the stinging darkness of his mother's puckered ways, like a buried seed waiting for the encouragements of spring.

Carol had become his spring. She was, to him, the triangular joy of trilliums that never pass.

This had become their annual rite, this appearance at the Iconic Wines Auction. It started as a single, thoroughly spiteful gesture: a bony middle finger raised in cultured defiance and stubborn pride, directed toward the unobservant and indifferent, toward the bitter parents who never failed to remind their unremarkable children of their failings, and how those shortcomings reflected poorly on the families, particularly on the mothers.

But then it became something more: a ritual. A sacred way, a path that pleaded to be taken again and again, because it promised renewed clarity with each passing. Bill and Carol agreed that whenever their humble circumstances allowed, this is what they would do for themselves, this tailored charade of theirs—tuxedoed and stockinged and scented and determined.

It was Lot #53 this time, one that would come up well near the end of the evening, but would hold the attention and interest of gentlemen in the front of the tinkling, murmuring ballroom in red. It would be the prize of the night.

An acclaimed bottle of Cain's Five 1985.

Several attendees wanted that blend of five varietal wines, but for the wrong reasons. For them it was the prestige. Or the tax write-off that the purchase price became as a charitable donation, and then the subsequent write-off the following year when that same bottle got donated back to the same auction with all the same bidders and the same fat man in a shiny red vest.

Carol and Bill knew the protocol. They knew what that bottle was actually worth, and how high others would go to get it. They knew, too, how much higher they themselves were willing to go to prove that a lifelong lack of any tangible talent did not preclude their ability to live virtuoso lives, in their own understated way. And so they bid.

"We open tonight at ten times the retail value," shouted Red Vest. "And there we have it. One thousand dollars from the gentleman in the distance. Now two. Now two. Now two."

A paddle flashed in the shadow of the auctioneer's belly.

"The game is on, Love," said Bill to Carol with a sly grin over his shoulder.

She looked up from her doodling to wink an acknowledgement, but quickly returned to her personal entertainment, content and confident.

"Two thousand dollars!" bellowed Red Vest. "Now three. Now three. Now three. Three! Three! Three! Yes! Number 228. Thank you, sir. Now four. Now four. Now four."

Bill glanced to Carol, asking her opinion with his earnest eyes.

"Wait just a bit more, Darling," she said. "Let them get their hopes up."

Bill stood his ground in the back of the ballroom, his paddle down but ready, his eyes frequently crossing paths with the vociferous auctioneer.

"Yes, yes, we have four thousand from the man to my right. Thank you, sir. Now five. Now five. Now five. Now five for this superlative blend made famous by the cool nights and short growing season of the Cain's mountain vineyard. FIVE IT IS! Now six. Now six. Now six. Now six. "

The auctioneer scanned the room for a red-coned flashlight but found none. The momentum of the bid had ebbed just as quickly as it had flowed. A bald man with Scorsese glasses began feeling a sense of ownership about lot #53, about that bottle of Cain's Five 1985, about how he'd display it on the credenza of his 33rd floor law office, how he might glance out his window at Mt. Hood as he explained the significance of his bidding victory to visiting clients, or how, if the right dining occasion came along, he might actually open that bottle for his successful buddies, pouring tastes of his treasure, opening the floodgates of his calculated generosity, metering out samples of his wonderful life.

"Now six. Now six. Now six."

It was time. Carol sensed it, and so put her doodling to rest. Bill knew as well.

"Only five? Only five?' asked the auctioneer. "Ladies and gentlemen, is this really the best the City of Roses can do tonight? Have we no pride in this fair city? Have we no shame?"

The question hung in the air high above the circular tables that obscured the flabby bellies and silken unmentionables of Portland's West Hills. They resigned from the fight en mass, signaling their answer, that the well-heeled and entitled of this village/city had only enough pride to get them by, and enough shame to last a lifetime.

Bill and Carol offered a different answer, though.

"SIX! From the gentleman in the distance. Number 531. Well done, sir. Well done."

Their mini-van did not suit their attire that night, but it suited Bill and Carol exquisitely. A white Toyota with sliding side doors. Utilitarian. More likely to be seen delivering cases of wine to restaurants than transporting a handsome couple home from an evening of indulgence.

Carol felt comforted by the sounds their mini-van made on the streets of Portland. By the muffled hum of tires on pavement. By the effortless whir of the engine. By the vibrations of motion and purpose, heightened by the sight of the man she loved at the wheel, humming a song beneath his breath.

Their neighborhood welcomed them home simply by existing. The newspaper box on the corner. The four-way stop at the quiet intersection. The bus bench. The utility poles holding the wires of commerce and convenience. The ancient drug store across the way. The dry cleaners with the clever sayings on the reader board. The locksmith. The wedding cake shop, which never wanted for young women with dreams and aging mothers with memories of what they had once dreamed for themselves.

It was nearly eleven when Bill and Carol pulled to a stop in front of their place, in the space reserved at all hours for deliveries. She got out carrying their prize. Bill got out carrying the two magnetic signs that, when secured on the sides of the mini-van, entitled them to park in front of the hardware store they owned and operated: Wingnuts & Whatnot. The name came with the business when they bought it, and they'd planned to change it. But by the time they took possession shortly after their marriage, and then moved into the simple apartment above the store, the silliness of the name gave way to an appreciation for the local color it represented, so the name lived on under their stewardship and in neon over their front door.

The deadbolt lock accepted Bill's key without complaint. The thumb trigger of the decades-old latch depressed smoothly, retracting the thing-a-ma-jig from the hearty strike plate on the opposing door, allowing them entry and sanctuary from their evening among those who might consider the hardware store a charming throwback from a quainter time.

This was no social experiment for Bill and Carol. This was simply what they chose.

Bill held the door for Carol, who smiled a thank you in exchange for his manners. He secured the deadbolt behind them and pulled the yellowing blind. The wooden floorboards squeaked and squawked as they walked the main aisle to the rear of the store, past the HELP counter, to the base of the stairs that led up to their mezzanine office. Carol took the railing in her hand, not because she needed steadying, but because she liked the feel of it and never missed the chance to touch it. Bill followed suit.

She lifted her long skirt just enough to allow her hips the room necessary to sit atop the desk, her legs dangling off the front. He pulled the widest drawer, retrieved their special bottle opener, and began the uncorking. Carol watched over her shoulder as Bill peeled the foil and burrowed the corkscrew; this job he took seriously, making sure to center himself in the cork, the gatekeeper of the Cain's Five 1985, their sacrificial wine.

"If anybody knew about this, they'd think we're nuts," said Carol. "You know that don't you?"

"Everybody's a little daft, Dear. Each of us in our own way."

"I suppose you're right. No, you are right. You really are. But still…"

"Oh now listen, Sweetheart. It's been years since either of us gave a bloody damn about what anybody else thinks. And prior to our respective epiphanies, we both spent far too much of our lives worrying about other people's expectations, great and small."

"Monumental expectations of the small-minded."

"Right then. What say we take this occasion to once again offer up a proper salute?" said Bill as he brought out two stunning wineglasses from a dark blue Swarovski box. "Let's show the old biddies what we're really made of, shall we? A little Caine Mutiny of our own?"

With that, he poured the wine from the bottle to the glasses, an equal inch in each. He walked around to the front of the desk and handed one to Carol, then he lifted his into the air between them. Carol lifted hers as well, still sitting. They looked into each other's eyes.

"Here's to personal truth, enormous love and the comeuppance of Machiavellian mothers everywhere," said Bill. "Because no matter how quickly we attain these treasures...."

"It's still a long time to be wrong," said Carol.

They sipped the wine. They smiled. Bill moved closer still, pausing within centimeters of Carol's lips. Then they kissed with a tenderness that could neither be measured nor matched.

"Now then, Love," said Bill as he stepped back to unleash his bow tie and shed his jacket. "Shall we complete this year's game of pretend? Shall I go first this time, or would you like the honor?"

"Please. You go ahead, Darling. I so love the way you tell it."

Bill cleared his throat with mock formality, retrieved his wine, and sat on the desk with Carol, scooting tight to her side, feeling warmth through her skirt.

"Right, then. Off I go."

Every bit and piece in the shadowy hardware store below the mezzanine railing awaited Bill's story. Every wingnut. Every coil of rope. Every woodscrew and roofing nail. Every snow shovel. Every little bristle of every perfect paintbrush. He took in a big breath, and then...

"I murdered my mother on the evening of May first, nineteen-sixty-seven."

"How ironic," said Carol with a coquettish grin. "Because as it happens, I murdered my mother as well. In nineteen-sixty-eight."

Pictures of Me

"Then why the hell do you keep doing it?" said Wanda St. Claire, her tight-cornered lips and crinkle-cornered eyes aimed away from her husband of thirty-one years, out the passenger-side window of their pickup truck, into the black of a moonless high desert. "I mean c'mon, Davis…it's damn near three in the morning and we're headin' for home. Our best friends kicked us out. They made us leave, Day. And I was already in bed, sound asleep!"

"He ain't my best friend no more," said Davis St. Claire slowly, his eyes shooting beams of self-righteousness down the centerline of the road, his voice in a bullfrog octave.

"I was 'sposed to make biscuits and gravy for everyone. Me and Rosie was 'sposed to hit that new antique mall. You and Charlie was 'sposed to go shoot sage rats."

"They'll do fine without us," said Davis, realizing that it would be a while before this fence got fixed, before there'd be breakfasts with Charlie and Rosie Booker again, before he'd be allowed to be around Rosie again, or her around him; his thick, inelegant hands ached from their fierce grip on the steering wheel.

"You know you're lucky I'm talkin' to you at all, Bub," said Wanda.

"Wouldn't bother me if you went on back to sleep," said Davis, instantly wishing he'd said something smarter—Wanda had sat there stone silent for the first seventy-five miles of desert highway, but he knew she'd start in eventually, that they'd have the talk, and that he'd come out of it poorly.

"You know what my brothers say about this business between you and Rosie?"

He lifted his eyes from the road to offer Wanda a laconic look in the almost-light of the dashboard that said *let me have it.*

"They been talkin' about it, you know. And they don't like it one damn bit. They way she sits in your lap all the time. The way you put your hands all over her right in front of everybody."

"Yeah." said Davis with his eyes locked ahead again.

"Yeah is right. And I told 'em both that it doesn't mean anything, and that I'm not worried in the least."

"But…"

"But they're not buying it," said Wanda. "And you know what, Day? There was a pause while they both let that unwelcome question hang there in the cab of the pick-up. Then… "I'm startin' to think maybe they gotta point."

"Well fuck me," said Davis indignantly.

"No, it's true. Maybe my little brothers got it right about you and Rosie. Maybe I oughta be pissed. Maybe Charlie and I DO have something to worry about. Do we, Day?

"I'm not gonna…"

Wanda never heard what it was that Davis wasn't going to do. What she heard instead was a hard flesh-on-metal smack at the front of the pick-up, then the instantaneous second smack of the windshield catching a weight that didn't belong. The deer's hoof shattered through and skewered the space between Wanda and Davis St. Claire, level with their eyes, flexing at the ankle as if to wave hello. Davis braked hard and blind, his view obliterated by the flailing animal, his headlights spraying everywhere but ahead, his tires digging into the knobby pavement, howling and smoking. They ended up sideways in the road.

Breathless.

Speechless.

Motionless.

Wanda felt warmth coming from the Pendleton wool seatcover beneath her, but was slow to understand that she'd peed herself. Davis sat rigid behind the wheel, still gripping it, his right leg twitching uncontrollably, his heart pounding in his smallish ears. The deer's hoof went slack and still: a graceful creature turned grotesque hood ornament.

The St. Claires smelled the details of it all. The pungent smoke of tires in friction with pavement. The rich, ripe gaminess of the buck's hind leg, ripped and scratched by glass, leaking blood and the musk of the mating season. The salty, misty quality of radiator fluid vaporizing on hot exhaust manifolds. The subtle scent of fresh urine.

Davis looked around the hoof at Wanda, whose round-faced features were awash in the clean white light of the now open glovebox. She felt his eyes and met them. Neither spoke. They just stayed locked on one another in resuscitation.

The engine was dead and quiet, save for the hissing and popping and gurgling of fluids.

A curtain call in the theatre of the unanticipated: the buck's carcass convulsed against the windshield. And before those venison reflexes fully subsided, the St. Claires found themselves afoot on the pavement in an instant act of flight. They continued to look at one another, now through the open doors of the pick-up.

Then Wanda broke off, walking toward the rear of the pick-up. Davis walked forward into akimbo headlights to assess things, but then immediately rejoined Wanda in the red glow of taillights. He dropped the tailgate and they both leaned their butts against it, to think.

"Guess we'd better move it off the road," said Davis flatly. "Just in case."

Neither budged. Not until Wanda finally took her weight off the tailgate and took a few steps into the dark, saying nothing. Davis got up, walked forward and climbed into the cab, cranked the ignition, and limped the pick-up to the crunchy shoulder; their Chevy could do no better.

The St. Claires knew without saying it aloud that they'd be waiting there until someone came along. There was nothing to walk to in either direction, and no way to phone. Davis would have to extract the buck from the windshield before rigormortise made the task even more difficult. Without anything to distract or divert them, they knew they'd continue the talk, trying to stay warm in the cab.

"So," said Wanda with an abruptness that made Davis' stomach juices squirt. "If you know how uncomfortable it makes everyone feel, how come you keep on doin' it?"

"Hell," said Davis in an effort to buy time, searching for resolve. "I sure don't know why everyone's got to be so damned sensitive all the time. Whada they call it now? Politically correct?"

"This ain't about political correctness, Day. This is about knowing when enough is enough. And maybe knowing the difference between foolin' around and *foolin' around.*"

"We's just havin' fun. Ain't nobody sneakin' around. Ain't nobody hidin' nothin' from anybody. Just like normal."

"And yet," interrupted Wanda, not appreciating his weak attempt at minimizing things. "Somehow you got Charlie so pissed at you tonight that we had to leave, and that sure as hell ain't normal."

Davis said nothing.

"So lay it out for me, Day. How come tonight turned out different? What'd you do after I went to bed?"

"Hell, Rosie went off to bed not ten minutes after you. And besides, it wasn't me that made things go all cock-eyed tonight. It was that damn Charlie, stupid son-of-a-bitch."

"Oh, that's rich. Blame it on Charlie."

"You damn right I blame it on Charlie, saying what he said."

"Which was?"

"Which was something he had no business sayin'. Not after everything I done for him. Not after all these years of me puttin' up with his braggin' and bullshittin' and drinkin' my whiskey every time we get together instead bringin' his own."

"What'd he say, Day?" said Wanda with no expectation of a miracle justification.

"It's just plain crazy."

"Uh-huh."

"Completely talkin' out his ass, that's for damn sure..."

"Davis."

He took a beat, not wanting to say it, and then…

"He accused me of bein' in love with Rosie."

Wanda let their talk come to a full stop upon hearing those words, giving that flatulent possibility time to dissipate in the air of the cab. It occurred to her that Charlie Booker might be onto something, and that she might look like very much the chump to have downplayed the concerns of her brothers. She let out a big sigh that fogged the glass.

"What," said Davis, now miles from the moral high ground.

Wanda sat in silence for another moment, then bent at the waist to reach for a Winston and the Zippo from her purse on the floorboard. She put the cigarette in her lips as she sat back and grabbed the door handle to exit the cab. Davis shot her a look of disapproval. But he could sense from the look he got back that his familiar protest wouldn't fly. *Not a fuckin' word,* said her eyes in the glovebox light.

It had been two decades since she last dared smoke in front of Davis, not wanting the grief, forever sneaking a drag here and there but never fully fooling him. She latched the door behind her. She flicked open the Zippo. Thumbed the tiny striker wheel. Made the spark that lit the white wick. Cupped the fluid flame. Lit the Winston. Snapped the Zippo closed. Took her first smoke. Crossed her arms before the second drag. Stood there—her back to Davis and their newest problem. And by the time she dropped that stubby cigarette butt to the pavement, it was clear to Wanda that this was the actual opportunity she'd been waiting and plotting for. To leave Davis. Again. Just like twenty-three years ago, only this time she could make it stick. He'd finally screwed up enough. It was a gift. An opportunity.

"Think big picture, honey," she said in a low, smokey voice that didn't carry back to the pick-up. "Big picture."

Seven Winstons later, the eastern sky was lighter than the west. Davis was asleep, slumped and snoring against the driver-side window. Wanda remained outside, favoring the chill of the desert air to the coldness she felt toward her red-nosed husband. She heard something coming and looked in the direction of the distant wind-rush. Finally, headlights crested.

A bronze Buick rolled to a stop right beside Wanda in the emerging predawn light. The passenger window lowered to reveal a white-haired couple, dressed for town and smiling like evangelists. Wanda could make out what looked like Jell-O salad under plastic wrap in the back seat, along with three pies; family reunion food, she figured. She saw, too, that the old folks had a CB radio. The man called on channel nine for help. The woman winked at Wanda as they pulled away, eager to make time and satisfied that they'd done enough.

Three months came and went before there was a word between the St. Claires and the Bookers. It was a notecard in the mail from Rosie to Wanda; blue ink in a graceful hand, no mention of the incident. Pretend it never happened, that was Rosie's naive meaning.

Wanda fingered the card at the kitchen table, her third cup of morning coffee steaming up beneath her chin. She was angry with herself for still being with Davis. For neither finding the courage nor seizing the moment. For gaining eleven pounds, too. He'd always ridden her hard about being heavy, but had held off since the big blowup. Wanda knew a shift was coming, though, and what had remained her advantage was about to evaporate like vapor off coffee.

Davis walked into the kitchen from the back porch with a curled piece of paper in his hand. He'd been out doing chores.

"Who's that from?" he said as he sat kitty-corner from Wanda at the table. "And what's for breakfast?"

She didn't answer right away, choosing instead to study the overlapping shadows of leaves dancing on the refrigerator door as the morning sunlight fingered into their kitchen, moving in and out of focus. The beauty of it was at odds with the tension.

"Coffee's hot. You're on your own if you want more."

Davis' chair squawked on the floor as he pushed back and stood up. He went to the cupboard in search of his favorite cup, but settled for his back-up. He filled it, added milk and put two slices of bread in the toaster.

"It's from your girlfriend," said Wanda without a hint of playfulness in her voice.

"Which one?"

"Pendleton."

Davis said nothing, knowing full well that the kitchen was suddenly as strewn with landmines as during his tour in Viet Nam. He was young then, and knew nothing of fear in the beginning. His mission had been simply to prove his father wrong: to show his smarts by coming home alive, and to thumb his nose at every landmine and boobytrap and mortar fragment and whiff of Agent Orange. If for no other reason than to defeat the memory of the old bastard back home. Davis could deal with most anything when he let his instincts take the point. But his wife was a challenge.

"What's that you brought in?" asked Wanda about the piece of heavy paper he'd left on the table, curled tight like a culvert.

"Somethin' I found out there in one my old boxes in the shed," he said as he buttered his toast at the counter. "A picture I forgot about."

"Picture of what?"

"Of a kid with his prize steer at the state fair."

"Oh yeah? Let's see," said Wanda as she picked up and uncurled the photo. "All these years and this is the first time I've ever seen this. What are you, ten? Twelve?"

"Eleven," said Davis. "Summer of '59. Inside the beef barn."

"Who's that with their back to the camera?"

"Pops."

"You look like you were crying."

"Yeah."

"Why?" asked Wanda, with roused compassion that instantly compromised her. She glanced over to Davis as he retook his seat at the table.

"The old man was giving me hell 'cause I hadn't got 'round to cleaning up the cow shit in the stall. He was telling me how lazy and stupid I was, and how embarrassed he was to claim me as his son. You know, the regular stuff."

"Oh, Day."

"I was just trying to get him to understand, but Pops wasn't much for listenin'."

He shrugged his shoulders as his took a bite of toast and then sipped his coffee. Wanda saw a lost look in his eyes.

"But didn't you ribbon that year? Don't we have it kickin' around here somewhere?"

"Second place," said Davis. "Which ain't fuckin' bad for a kid going against grownups."

"Second place is great. But wait, who took the picture? And who in their right mind would give a kid a picture of themselves crying, in the middle of an argument with their dad, smack in the middle of the state fair?"

"Oh, I think it was someone working for the fair. Some college punk with a camera. Sent it to Mom afterward, thinking she'd appreciate how *honest* it was. That's what she said, anyway."

"Did she?"

"She was glad to have a picture of me and Pops together," said Davis as his finished his toast. "But she said it made her sad to see me so sad."

He continued with his coffee, and she with hers. The dancing leaves on the refrigerator were gone, leaving the St. Claires no choice but to find some sort of grace on their own. Davis turned sideways in his chair, his legs no longer beneath the table, his arm hooked over the back of the chair, his back now mostly toward Wanda. She remained motionless over her cup, both elbows heavy against the table. Outside, a truck passed by on the road along the front of the place. The refrigerator clunked in a way so familiar that neither of them heard it. Nor did they register the muffled click-click-click of the battery-powered clock on the wall.

"I used to be good," said Davis in a voice so small, Wanda could barely recognize it. "I used to be a good person. A long time ago."

"Davis?"

"I know it's true, Wanda. Because I saw it in pictures of me when I was a little guy."

"This picture you mean? You and your dad at the fair?"

"This picture, sure. And other pictures, too. In the albums I got from Mom when she died. And it's all proof that I started out good. People used to tell Mom they wished their kids could be like me. Hard worker. Did what I was told. Looked for ways to help. Never lied. Never sassed my dad, even when he was mean from drinkin' and pissed at everyone."

"Why are you telling me this, Day? What's going on here?

Davis lifted his cup to take a full swallow that emptied it. His throat gurgled through the flesh of his neck. Wanda watched his Adam's apple slide up and down as he looked away through the kitchen windows and then back at her. She saw that his eyes were suddenly wet, which prompted hers to become the same. He tried to speak but only managed a staccato breath. He tried again and failed again.

"I'm too old to be doing this," he thread-whispered. "I been lacin' up my boots too damn long. Kept thinkin' I'd outgrow it."

"Oh Sweetheart, what are you talking about here? Huh? Outgrow what?"

"This feeling."

"Tell me about it, so I can understand. Can you tell me?"

Davis dropped his head and fixed his eyes on a paperclip on the floor between his feet. He bent to retrieve it between his thumb and forefinger. He placed it on the table beside his cup.

"No, I don't think I can," said Davis, feeling confident that he'd wrangled enough sympathy from Wanda to finally put the Rosie trouble to rest.

The phone rang seven times in Charlie Booker's welding shop before he could get there to answer it with soiled hands. The bandana he wore on his bald head was wet with sweat. The coveralls he wore to protect his skin from molten metal were pocked with burn holes. The mood of the moment was good, because he'd just mastered a very tricky weld on a broken hay baler.

"Booker Welding," he announced into the mouthpiece.

"It's me," said the woman's voice in his ear.

"Wanda?"

"How's it goin?"

"It's goin' okay, Baby. How's it goin' down there?"

Wanda took a beat before answering.

"Not so good, I'm afraid. Not so good."

"Whadaya mean not so good?"

"I mean, it's not gonna happen, Charlie. I can't go through with it."

"You gotta be kiddin' me."

"Nope."

"So you're sayin' what…we're done, me and you?"

"Yep."

"Just like that?"

"Just like that, Charlie. I'm sorry."

A pause, and then…

"I can't believe it."

"It was a crazy idea, Charlie. We were crazy to even try it. Settin' Davis and Rosie up like that. Letting 'em do our dirty work. Just plain crazy."

"Huh," said Charlie digesting the news. He pulled the soggy bandana off of his head and wiped his brow. He let out a big sigh as he considered what to do or say next.

"I gotta get back to work, Wanda. On deadline for a fella. Talk to ya later."

He hung up the phone and returned to the hay baler. He studied his weld, the way the layers folded onto one another with near-perfect spacing, how the weld shined in the fluorescent shop lights. He wondered what Rosie would make for supper that night. He wondered whether he'd be able to stay in the same room with her long enough to eat it.

"Helluva deal, buddy," he said to himself with a disapproving and judgmental tone. "Ya stupid son-of-a-bitch."

Rosie made meatloaf on the evening of Booker's success with the broken hay baler.

She'd worked hard to get it right, understanding that it was one of his new favorites, and later watched out the corner of her eye as he forked and chewed it, wishing her husband was better looking. Or more interesting. Or a better dancer. Or at least funny. Something.

The recipe came from a woman who read Tarot cards. It was a gift. A thank-you; the traveling card reader's way of showing appreciation for the twenty-five dollar fee, and for helping her clients feel better after getting bad news in the back seat of her bronze Buick.

The car had been sitting in the Pendleton Safeway's parking lot not long after the blowup with the St. Claires. A piece of cardboard stuck in the windshield advertised TAROT READINGS. The white-haired couple sat in folding chairs in the dismal shade of an unhealthy tree in the perimeter landscaping; he whittled on a stick and whistled, while she knitted and listened.

Rosie wanted her future told in plain terms. She wanted particulars. Something to help her make sense of the confusions that dogged her, such as why she kept finding herself in Davis St. Claire's lap when the four of them got together to party. Why she acted as if she liked his coarse hands on her diminutive legs and hips and belly. Why she giggled when in fact she was sad. Why she was too weak to come clean about all of it.

The white-haired woman spoke in a way that was every bit as circular as the cards she used, the two of them in the back of the Buick, the doors open for crosswind, a thick piece of cardboard on the seat between the women to serve as a table. She spoke of ungraceful times, then the struggle for abundance, and then the vague suggestion of betrayal. She spoke of cups and major arcana and screw-you cards. And at the precise moment that the card reader touched on the topic of romance, a helicopter passed over the Safeway, its rotors chopping away at any chance Rosie had of hearing what she most wanted to know.

Rosie came away unsatisfied. Not a lick of it seemed worth the twenty-five bucks, so she was glad to at least get a decent meatloaf recipe on a white three-by-five card with faint blue lines. At least that was useful.

Later, when she was unpacking groceries at home, Rosie noticed something on the back of the recipe card. A hand-written note in pencil:

> *Wanda will never be yours. So make do, dear. Make meatloaf. Many a marriage has been saved by less!*

Barefoot with Rita

I love the smell of burning bridges. At least that's what my adoptive parents say about me. And I wouldn't be at all surprised to learn that pretty much everyone I've ever known or been in close contact with would say the same thing. Which only goes to show the extent to which I have been misunderstood.

It's a shame, really. An injustice. Because if you take the time necessary to know the real me, well, you'll see that Robin McAllister really isn't all that bad.

For one thing, I'm very attractive. Take my word, I'm not one of those women who wakes up ugly and then spends an hour in front of the mirror repairing the deficiencies of nature. Many people have told me I wake up looking gorgeous, and I'm not in much of a position to disagree. Because even after a long and adventuresome night out, I look like a

Barbie right out of the box. Pretty as ever and no worse for the wear.

My eyes are a beautiful shade of blue in the morning. A deep violet blue that skews toward indigo as the day goes on. Looking into my eyes, it's clear why I have such an affect on people in general, and men in particular. Seriously. They can't help themselves in the least. That's how unavoidably beautiful Robin McAllister's eyes are. Of course I use an appropriate amount of eyeliner and mascara to make the most of what I've got. That's mostly to satisfy myself. Although sometimes, I dial it up to accomplish a special task. You know, to win somebody over. Somebody I want something from. Then my eyes are roadblock beautiful.

But maybe you're not all that interested in my devices. So let me tell you about my nose. Basically, it's perfect. Small, of course. And symmetrical in shape, which the fashion magazines say is an essential component of true beauty. People like perfect symmetry. I read one article about how these psychologists conducted a study with little babies to see how they reacted to women with symmetrical facial features versus women with unbalanced faces. It came as no surprise to me that the babies were drawn to the symmetrical women. I've seen it my whole life. People of all ages are simply drawn to me at first sight. You can see it in their eyes. It's as if they go into some sort of trance or something. Crazy. Anyway, back to my nose. My nostrils are discreet. And thank God they aim fully toward the ground. Because I just hate it when someone's got nostrils that point right at you. Always reminds me of the air intake on jet engines. I mean, it can be frightening. But no one's ever going to get the creeps from *my* nostrils. And they're never going to see anything unsightly there either. I make sure of that. It's a rule I have. Now the last thing I have to say about my nose is that I have small pores. So the complexion thing isn't a problem. Nor is it a problem anywhere else on my face, which is also perfectly symmetrical.

My cheekbones, for instance, are high and pronounced. People are always commenting on them, saying things like I have the makings of a model. No surprise there. But what always gets me is how consistently people go from complimenting my cheekbones to complimenting my smile. It's almost like everybody got advanced notes on the proper order of compliments to be paid to Robin McAllister, so as not to annoy me or disrupt the natural rhythm of my day.

The teeth are good, as you might guess. Bright and big, with the kind of alignment that everyone hopes for but few people have.

My finest feature, though, could well be my lips. They're big and full, and really nice to kiss. They're the kind of lips that can close the deal. One woman friend called them pillow lips. And she would know. Because—now I'm sorry if you find this shocking—there was a time when we spent plenty of pillow time together. These days, though, I have nothing to do with her and nothing more to say about her. She had her chance.

Maybe you've noticed that I haven't described my hair, or my body. Well there's a reason for that. And all I'm going to say is that my hair has been many colors and styles, and it all works for me. As for the rest of me, let's just skip it.

I am 37. I live in the Greater Salt Lake City area with my husband, Donny, and my three boys. Donny works in the promotions department for the Utah Jazz, which means I'm one of the semi-regulars in the courtside seats, although it's rarely the same seat. I had hoped when we first got married that Donny could manage to secure a regular seat that would position me opposite the Jazz bench, so I could make eye contact with the players. But it turned out that Donny didn't have all that much weight in the organization. So I've had to make do with this seat and that one. The important thing is that I get my fair share of face time during televised games. The cameras love me, you know. Because most of them are operated by men.

I've been pushing Donny to buy one of those impressive Salt Lake City homes that back right up to the mountains on the way to the ski resorts, where all the players have places. But Donny is reluctant. So when the games are over and the television lights go dark, we have to drive all the way down to American Fork, which most people consider part of the Greater Salt Lake City area.

Sometimes I wonder about Donny. About his ambition. Because it's starting to feel like he'd be happy just staying in American Fork with the rest of his massive Mormon family. Now there's a dull bunch. They pitch a fit if one of them sees me drinking a Coke, whether or not there's rum involved. And to top it off, half of his siblings sing in the Mormon Fishin' Tackle Choir. Which is what I call it when nobody's listening.

Donny makes okay money, I suppose. He's handsome. Keeps the front yard looking sharp. Gets free Delta tickets through the Jazz. Looks good in a tux. And for what it's worth, he's pretty good with the boys, considering none of them are his. (Although he thinks the youngest one is his.) But I'm certain life's got something better in store for me, and that I'm entitled to whatever it is.

That's why you find me here in one of Delta's finest first class seats, winging my way back to Salt Lake from my first visit to New York City. I went there on a mission. And if you think you can give my story the serious attention it warrants, I'll tell you about that right now.

But understand, I take this business very seriously. And I'm feeling pretty raw about the whole thing.

After months of research in the genealogy department of the Mormon Church, I pretty much confirmed the identity of my birth mother. She lives and works in New York City. So I went there to meet her in person.

Adopted kids do this sort of thing all the time, I know. But my situation is unique. Because my mother is famous. In fact, she's one of the few performers ever to win an Oscar, a Tony, a Grammy and an Emmy. And here's the really weird thing about it: I loved her before I knew she was my mom, and I've always been her biggest fan.

I've been writing to her for years. I know everything about her. I've seen every movie she's ever made. I've read reviews of every Broadway production she's ever been in. I even got to watch her on Sesame Street and on reruns of the Rockford Files. So it was quite a revelation when I discovered she also happened to be my mother. Quite a lucky day.

After all, who else can claim to be the illegitimate daughter of Rita Moreno?

There must be a terrific story to be told about me. About my secret birth in some undisclosed location. About the doctors and nurses who vowed silence at the behest of Rita Moreno herself.

And there was the question of paternity. Who is my real father? An actor? A director? A producer? I get chills just thinking about it. And this is just part of what I hoped to learn about on this trip back east. Because I have to confess, she's never answered any of my letters. Not even after I sent her pictures of me, so that she could see the resemblance.

I flew into Newark just yesterday. Being early November and all, the trees of New Jersey actually looked kind of pretty in the sunset as we circled the airport. Nobody ever told me New Jersey had trees. So it came as a pleasant surprise. And it made me feel as though this whole New York adventure might not be as intimidating as I had imagined.

The town car I took into Manhattan was right out of Seinfeld, complete with a pasty, sweaty white guy at the wheel. He could be a real butt, I'm sure. But it didn't take him long to realize that I was worthy of his respect. So he was a prince the whole way in, even when things got a little tense entering the New Jersey Tunnel, where eight lanes of traffic came down to two, and people were using their horns like swords.

Next thing I knew, we squirted out the other end of that dingy, tiled tunnel and into Manhattan. The sun had disappeared in the time it took to get this far. But I quickly realized that New York City doesn't get its vitality from natural light, which I also found oddly reassuring.

Shooting across Times Square in traffic was a bright, brilliant blur. But I'm pretty sure I saw some famous things.

Then my driver took me up West 44th Street. He drove slowly here, because the street had narrowed. Everywhere I looked there were couples and four-somes getting out of taxis and town cars and limousines, and they were all going into theatres. The marquees were huge and dazzling. And very close to me.

That's what really struck me about that happy, clean street with all the theatres. The intimacy. The proximity of the big time and the bright white lights.

I felt as though I was in a parade. It seemed as if the people of Manhattan had come out to welcome Robin McAllister. And to let me know that this city wasn't as bad as it seemed. And that there was room for me here. And that they understood the significance of my arrival, not to mention the importance of establishing contact with my famous mother.

I was pleased by all of this.

The last time I got near a parade, it was an awful scene. It was back in Brookings, the Southern Oregon coastal town made famous by meteorologists for its unusually warm climate.

My first husband, Kurt, was the second assistant chief of the volunteer fire department. Which meant it was his duty to appear as Santa Claus in the annual holiday parade. That was the tradition in Brookings.

Kurt was a desperately handsome man. He adored me with special vigor. And he helped me conceive my first son. But he dressed poorly, and wasn't worried about what people thought. Which helps explain why he decided Santa should drive a cherry red dune buggy in the parade, a sand rail if you want to be technical, rather than simply riding atop the fire truck.

I was set to ride with him as Mrs. Claus. And I'd even gone to the bother of getting Kurt's mother to make me a cute little Mrs. Santa suit, complete with fluffy white trim along the hem of a very short but billowy skirt. But on his way from the fire station to where the parade was forming, he got T-boned by a bronze Buick. Thank God I wasn't with him yet.

His buddies had quite a time dealing with the Santa suit as he lay sprawled on the pavement, because the blood was hard to spot. But they managed to gather Santa up and haul him to the hospital.

Fine, I thought. I'll go to the damn hospital. Never mind the parade, I thought. Never mind my outfit. Let's go be with Kurt in the hospital. Let's go be compassionate. Why not? I'm certainly not going to be riding in any parade today, I thought. Just fine!

Kurt came out of it okay. You know, a broken neck that healed and amnesia that lasted for months. Not too bad, really.

But after a year of nursing him back to health, I'd come to the realization that being the dutiful wife of the second assistant fire chief of Brookings, Oregon was simply not going to be enough. And that in his reduced condition, Kurt was increasingly worthless to me. So the day before he was once again set to ride in the holiday parade, I marched out of Brookings with my infant son.

It was for the best.

My travel agent had booked me into the Algonquin Hotel, which was easy to spot amid the beautiful white lights of West 44th. As the town car pulled up to put my door handle within reach of the Algonquin's doorman, I wondered if anybody on the street thought I might be somebody important. It seemed to me that people were staring.

The lobby of the Algonquin was charming. The colors were rich and warm, the lighting was subdued but by no means dark, and the ornate ceiling was quite high. I liked the way the furniture was situated, with all sorts of high-backed arm chairs and interesting sofas, all arranged in little conversation clusters, most of which were occupied by well-dressed people drinking cocktails and talking.

The lobby waiters were dressed in black waistcoats, black slacks, white shirts, and black bow ties. They all carried silver serving trays, and were constantly in motion.

I noticed that when they took an order, the waiters disappeared through a discreet doorway in the dark paneling that surrounded the lobby people. A small sign above the door offered a clue.

The Blue Bar.

I asked the man checking me in if that's where Rita Moreno performs. Because I had not gone to the Algonquin by accident. (I don't do anything by accident.) I had done my research. And I'd learned that The Algonquin Hotel had one of the last true cabarets in New York City. And that this was where my unsuspecting mother would be performing her one-woman show.

"No," answered the desk clerk without looking up at me. "That's the Blue Bar. Miss Moreno does her show in the Oak Room, back there." He gestured to the rear of the lobby, toward a pair of closed double doors I had not noticed. "If you want tickets, just call our cabaret ticket office from your room. They'll help you," he said.

Then the desk clerk proceeded to ramble on about the history of the hotel. He made a big deal about that stupid Round Table, which was located just inside the dining area in the very back of the lobby. But I had not come to New York for the sake of a bunch of dead writers who drank too much. I was there to meet someone important. Someone to whom I'd written some of my most private thoughts.

I immediately booked a table for two for the following night's show. Then, after freshening up a bit, I went back down to the Blue Bar for an Absolut Citron and tonic. And to find the companion I'd need for the cabaret show.

The Blue Bar was smaller than I expected. The dark wood paneling was crafted into large geometric squares, with lots of ornate trim work. Tiny wall-mounted lights lined the room but barely created any light beyond their respective square on the wall. The light was as low and smoky as the conversations of the murmuring couples tucked here and there. They were all dressed in black, and hardly anyone even seemed to notice me in my backless blue dress. The bartender noticed, of course. But he seemed irritated by my presence, and spoke to me in a very clipped foreign accent that was courteous, but impatient. I smiled sweetly when he brought my drink and then cursed his existence as he shuffled away.

I noticed through the discreet windows facing the street that it had begun to rain, which doused any notions I'd had about venturing out into midtown Manhattan that night. Better, I thought, to sit tight in the Algonquin and take my chances in the Blue Bar, useless bartender and all.

Three Absoluts and a Caesar salad later, it occurred to me that nothing good would come of this dreary little place. I'd begun to feel as though I'd become part of a pen-and-ink cartoon drawn for the pages of some snooty magazine. I felt surrounded by caricatures of unsmiling New Yorkers. And somewhere in the room, someone was saying something that was intensely clever but completely understated. And someone else was looking over the top of their dry martini with one eyebrow raised in response to what they'd overheard. And the unpleasant bartender discreetly rolled his eyes toward the dark ceiling as if to say he thought he'd heard it all. And me? I was the beautiful woman alone at the end of the bar, my lack of understanding as exposed as my back.

Losers. That's all I could think. I was in a room full of useless losers who didn't know or care about what I was up against. To hell with them, I thought. To hell with finding a date to balance out my table at the Rita Moreno show. To hell with everything. And by the way, if you don't like me or what I'm about, to hell with you. Okay?

That's how it is, you know? Every now and again, people need to be told to go to hell. It's a cleansing process for me. A ritual. I find someone that's worthwhile, and I let them get close. I get what I can. And then, when the goodness plays out, they're out.

Maybe this seems harsh. But you sure can't argue with my results.

After all, I've got three little boys who love me for all they're worth. That's something, isn't it? And there's my education. A Bachelor of Science degree with a Geology major from Humboldt State University.

It's kind of funny when you think about it; how I went from spending weekends on the sand dunes with Kurt to spending weekends in the library studying rocks. And how I'd managed to get pregnant with my second son by discovering bedrock with the head of the Geology Department. His name was

Ian. A full professor with a full-blown British accent. Which makes sense considering he grew up in a small village just outside of Northhamptonshire, England.

Ian wanted badly to marry me, which was sweet. He tried every thing he could think of, too. Money for tuition and living expenses. Good grades. A nice little used Saab to drive. He even managed to set me up with a scholarship while I was there, the ceremony for which resulted in a photo and story in the student newspaper.

But here was the problem with Ian.

He loved it there in Arcata, California. He loved the weather. He loved the coastal plain that reaches out from the town to the beach itself. He loved those weather-beaten farms that line the tidal rivers. He loved the bridges of Arcata. But most of all, and this is the part that really killed me; he loved the people there. Because they reminded him of his people back home. People who live in the mist and gray. People who can go for days without sunshine. People who can drink all night to get over the dreariness of their day, and then get right up the next morning and proceed as if they had something to look forward to in life. Ian loved that dedication to nothingness.

Me? I liked two things about Arcata. Getting my degree, and spending weekends in my favorite little seaside resort town, Trinidad, where weekenders from San Francisco congregate. Other than that, the place had nothing for me.

So about a month after graduation, my two boys and I took off. But not before I'd secured my second son's financial future by threatening to reveal Ian's tryst with me to the university. He hated the very idea of blackmail. But he could afford a small trust fund for my son far more than he could afford a scandal.

I made a mistake in Arcata, though. I'd left too soon. Because I was two weeks down the road when I realized I was once again pregnant. There was no way to pin it on Ian. And time was short. So I headed for the nearest place I knew of where large families are considered a good thing. A status symbol, even.

Utah!

On my way from the Blue Bar to the lobby elevator, I noticed a cat on the front desk. Cats like me. I strolled over to say hello.

"Our cat seems to be taken with you, Ma'am," said a smooth baritone voice from over by the main entrance. It was the doorman.

"Yes," I said without turning around to him. "There's just something about me."

"In town for a show, Ma'am?"

"Well as a matter of fact, yes. The Rita Moreno show. Right here in the cabaret. Have you heard good things?"

As I asked the question, I turned fully to face the short but striking black man in a burgundy uniform with gold trim. But the weird thing was, he immediately looked as if he recognized me. As if we'd met somewhere before.

"You're Miss McAllister, aren't you?"

"Why yes," I replied. "That's me. How'd you know?"

The doorman hesitated. Then he explained that it's the Algonquin's policy for the entire staff to become familiar with the guests, and whenever possible, to greet people by name. It's hospitality protocol, he said.

I went up to my room and then to bed. I drifted off thinking how nice it was to be recognized in the hotel lobby in New York City on my very first visit, and to be liked by cats. I thought about what I planned to say to Rita the next evening down in the Oak Room. I thought about how she might receive me. I thought about her giving me a huge hug right there in front of everyone. I thought about us crying together, and then seeing the episode retold on Entertainment Tonight. And with that, I slept well.

I awoke the next morning looking unruffled, as usual. But I was unsettled. Because I'd managed, up to that point, to go without actually setting foot on the streets of Manhattan. And I knew how stupid it would be to spend the whole day in the hotel, waiting to see Rita. So I resolved myself to a plan to overcome my angst.

Dressed and full of anxious energy, I stepped from the elevators into the bustle of the lobby during the morning checkout. I maneuvered through the luggage and long-coated people to the front doors, which swung open at the hands of a doorman I hadn't seen before. Oddly, and very much like the other doorman, he recognized me.

"Good morning, Miss McAllister."

"Good morning," I said, thinking again how nice it was to be acknowledged.

But let's get down to business, I told myself. Let's take a hard right turn out the door and immediately begin walking. Let's match the pace of everyone going the same direction. Let's not look anybody in the eye. And most important of all, I told myself, let's not let anybody see my fear. Let's act completely unimpressed with everything and everyone. No matter what. If you can manage that, I encouraged myself, you'll be fine.

And I was.

When I came to the corner of West 44th and Fifth Avenue, I resolved to continue on around the block. Within minutes, I found myself approaching the entrance to the Algonquin from the opposite direction.

I'd made it. Mission accomplished, I thought. Good job, Robin. Step on inside and reward yourself with coffee in the lobby. Sit in the high-backed chair with purple upholstery and gold piping, the one that lets you see the whole room. And when the server in black and white scurries up, go ahead and order yourself a bagel to go with your well-deserved coffee. Or a croissant, maybe.

As I waited for the return of the faceless little man with the silver tray, time-delayed impressions of the streets outside streamed through my mind.

There was no sky. Only buildings that seemed to grow together at the top, where the sky should be. Gray buildings. Concrete. Glass. People dressed mostly in black or shades of black.

There were no bad smells. Only the scent of bacon when I passed by delis and cafés. And coffee when I went past the Starbucks. And perfume on women who, when they stopped to wait for the crosswalk light, probably enjoyed their own scents.

There were no street people. No panhandlers. No bums. Only well-dressed people with places to go. Or delivery truck men who seemed at ease with themselves. Or frantic food vendors, who sold donuts and fruit to people who were not yet fully awake or ready to talk.

There was nothing to be afraid of. And upon accepting that fact, I decided to spend the day wandering. But first, I returned to my room to put on something black.

November in Manhattan. People of all colors dressed in black. Rich people shopping on Madison Avenue. Athletic people jogging though Central Park. Talkative people in chic restaurants, waiting to see or be mistaken for somebody famous. Yellow cabs everywhere. But more than anything, people. So many it made my head swim and my feet hurt. Such a temptation it was to look up where the sky should have been. Such an unwavering urge there was to look passers-by in the eye. But such a source of personal pride it was to do neither, to keep pressing on with false purpose and a jaded face. And to do so with such conviction that I caused tourists to comment on my New York rudeness as I brushed past them, importantly. Look out, losers, I said to myself. I'm Robin McAllister. And this is *my* town now.

But as I tired, it came to me that this was actually my birth mother's town. And that I'd do well to remember that fact. So off I went to the Algonquin. To prepare for my big evening.

Brushing past my courtly doorman and toward the cat that was sniffing luggage, it came to me that I should get an advance look at the Oak Room. So that I could enter the show with confidence, looking completely comfortable with my surroundings. Like a regular.

The double doors to the Oak Room were closed but not locked. Nobody noticed me slipping in.

The house lights were up and the Oak Room was empty. It turned out to be nothing more than an extension of The Blue Bar. With the same dark, square panels on the walls. And the same tiny light fixtures running the length of the rectangular room on both sides. The ceiling was much higher, though. More like it is out in the main lobby. Affixed to the ceiling were several rows of small but I'm sure powerful spotlights, all aimed at the grand piano that was situated in the middle of the room, against the wall. In front of the piano was a small area of wood parquet flooring, where Rita no doubt sings, leaning against the piano, chatting with her pianist and her audience. The carpeted portion of The Oak Room was crowded with small, round tables, each with two chairs. Along the wall opposite the piano was a row of even smaller tables with one chair each.

Stepping onto the parquet, I imagined being there with Rita. She in a sparkling dress in the spotlights. Me in my blue dress seated within her view, illuminated by my table's candle.

I imagined her performing her first set. Maybe something from Rogers and Hammerstein. Or Blizzard of Lies. Or maybe The New York City Blues.

I pictured Rita Moreno smiling the smile that years earlier had won over Louis B. Mayer. And her beautiful brown eyes; I could see them vividly, and I appreciated how they managed to hold Brando's attention for all those years.

I conjured up my mother floating around the room in dance. Her body still trim and fit and graceful. Just as she was as a 16-year-old nightclub dancer, playing the Latin Spitfire for all her worth. Or later, as she was earning her Oscar for Anita in West Side Story.

I sat there under the unpleasant fluorescent lights with respect for Rita, the former Rosita. A little Puerto Rican girl who grew up like me, shy and inadequate, but who made it to Broadway by age 13. I sat there alone and cried at the thought of how it must have killed her to play all those typecast parts. The hot-blooded Latin sex kitten. And how she played those parts barefoot, with her nostrils flaring, her blouse off her shoulders, her hoop earrings swaying, her teeth gnashing. Doing what she had to do to win. Just like me.

I sighed out loud.

"You're not supposed to be in here," said the baritone voice.

I turned toward the door. It was the first doorman who'd recognized me. He was leaning in the double doors of The Oak Room, and he was looking far less pleasant than when opening the main doors of the Algonquin's lobby.

"Oh, yes. I belong here," I said. "But I'll go if you answer a simple question for me."

"Quickly, Miss McAllister."

"What time should I plan on being seated for Rita Moreno?"

I did not like the answer.

"Cancelled."

"Cancelled?!" I shouted.

"Yes, Miss McAllister. And if I may be blunt, you of all people should understand why Miss Moreno's people decided she shouldn't perform tonight. Anyway, everyone gets a refund. With the Algonquin's apologies, of course."

"Of course!"

The only thing I understood was my outrage. My face and neck instantly felt hot and painful. My fingers and feet felt ice cold. There was a high-pitched ringing in my ears. I vaulted from the patch of parquet floor, past the frowning doorman and into the lobby, directly into the path of a stupid little waiter. The silver tray and coffee service he was delivering found its way to the floor with such speed and intensity that I don't recall hearing what must have been a loud crash, or the instant hush that must have consumed the lobby guests. I do recall the sight, however, of coffee and cream and sugar in a splatter pattern on the floor, and a picture of me amongst the mess. A picture I'd had taken back in Brookings.

It was the first thing retrieved by the waiter. And though it was puzzling that the waiter carried a picture that I had sent to Rita Moreno with one of my many letters, I was too upset by the cancellation and the collision to think about it. The elevator opened and I exited the scene.

I immediately began to pack. Then I phoned Delta to get an earlier flight back to Salt Lake City. Robin McAllister had had enough of New York City. And with Manhattan, in particular. An overrated chunk of land surrounded by two straits and an estuary that they jokingly refer to as rivers. Life's too short, I thought. At least the Great Salt Lake is honest about what it is. A big, salty lake. And while it can't support fish life any better than the Hudson, Harlem and East rivers, at least we've got our brine shrimp. At least there's that.

The next available flight was in three hours. So I checked out. And my last impression of the Algonquin was seeing their damned lobby cat sound asleep on the back counter of the registration desk, its tail draped across a short, neat stack of photocopies of my picture. Fuck the Algonquin, I thought.

I've never liked the looks of Delta's fleet. But when you sit in first class, it's not such a bad airline. Not really. And today, having failed in my quest to meet my mother as I'd planned, I have a sense of gratitude to the airline whose planes I see coming and going all day in Utah. The flight attendants are nice to me, and generous with the vodka, too. They make it comfortable. They allow me time and space to think. To work it out in my head. To get this whole unfortunate incident squared away, just as I have had to do so many times before.

But listen, enough of that. Because the man across the aisle keeps looking over at me. And he looks like somebody I think I've seen on TV. And the tag on his carry-on says NBC Sports. And the seat beside him is as empty as the one beside me. And, well, I just got an idea.

ABOUT THE AUTHOR

DAN T. COX WAS BORN in 1953 in Corvallis, Oregon. He grew up in Oregon's North Santiam Canyon, earned a journalism degree from the University of Oregon, became part of Portland's advertising creative community, and now lives in Ridgefield, Washington. His short fiction has appeared in literary journals such as *Weber Studies* and *Skyline*. *A Bigger Piece of Blue* is his debut book.

www.dantcox.com

CPSIA information can be obtained
at www.ICGtesting.com
Printed in the USA
FSHW04n1251120418
46905FS